Ronald Mackin · John Eastwood

A Grammar of Spoken English

Cornelsen & Oxford University Press

A Grammar of Spoken English wurde verfaßt von

Ronald Mackin, M.A., Colchester
John Eastwood, M.A., Street/Somerset

unter beratender Mitarbeit von

Rainer Diebschlag, Dorsten
Edgar Dietz, Weil am Rhein
Ulrike Florath, Hagen
Burkhart Nather, Mülheim/Ruhr
Hartmut von Roden, Witten

Redaktion: Dr. Rolf Schneider; Fritz Preuß

1. Auflage 1980

Bestellnummer 5488

Druck: CVK-Druck, Berlin

ISBN 3-8109-0548-8

Vertrieb: Cornelsen-Velhagen & Klasing Verlagsgesellschaft, Bielefeld

Inhaltsverzeichnis

		Page
Vorwort		4
1	Word order	5
2	Verbs: Talking about the present	7
3	Verbs: Talking about the past	12
4	Verbs: Talking about the future	20
5	Verbs: *be, have* and *do*	24
6	The imperative and *let's*	28
7	Modal verbs	29
8	Negatives, questions and tags	38
9	Replacing words and leaving out words	42
10	The passive	44
11	If-clauses	49
12	Reported speech	51
13	Tenses in main clauses and sub clauses	55
14	The infinitive	56
15	The -ing form	61
16	The infinitive and the -ing form	63
17	The -ing form and the -ed form	65
18	Nouns	68
19	The articles: *a/an* and *the*	74
20	Pronouns and quantifiers	79
21	Question words	91
22	Relative clauses	93
23	Adjectives	98
24	Adverbs	103
25	Prepositions	112
26	Verbs with adverbs and prepositions	115
27	Conjunctions and other linking words	118
28	Emphasis	122
29	Word-building	125
30	The pronunciation and spelling of endings	129
31	Numbers, money etc	131
32	Communication: Starting and finishing a conversation	134
33	Communication: Statements and opinions	137
34	Communication: Telling and asking people to do things	139
35	Communication: Feelings	144
36	Communication: Right and wrong	146
37	Punctuation	147
38	Weak forms and short forms	151
39	Stress and intonation	152
40	List of common irregular verbs	153
Index		154
Glossary		159

Vorwort

Diese Grammatik ist ein Buch zum Nachschlagen, Lernen und Wiederholen. Will man eine Sprache verstehen und sprechen lernen, hilft es nicht, Regeln auswendig zu wissen. Das Hauptgewicht liegt daher in diesem Buch auf den Beispielsätzen, aus denen ganz klar hervorgeht, was man in der modernen Umgangssprache sagt oder schreibt, und wie man es sagt. Darunter stehen Anmerkungen zur Form, also dazu, wie eine grammatische Struktur gebildet wird, und zur Anwendung. Diese durch unterschiedliche farbige Hervorhebung gegliederten Anmerkungen erklären, worum es sich bei den Beispielen in den Kästen handelt und wie eine grammatische Struktur gebraucht wird.

Schon nach zwei Jahren Englischunterricht kann mit dieser Grammatik und mit Anmerkungen in englischer Sprache gearbeitet werden. Die Fähigkeit, korrekte Aussagen darüber zu machen, wie grammatische Strukturen gebildet und angewandt werden, erwirbt man leichter, wenn man dazu die englische Sprache benutzt. So werden Fehler, die sich aus dem Gebrauch der Muttersprache ergeben, vermieden.

Die grammatischen Strukturen wurden nach der Häufigkeit des Vorkommens und nach der Nützlichkeit für den Lernenden ausgewählt. Enthalten sind auch einige vielleicht nicht so häufige Strukturen, die man aber erkennen sollte, damit es nicht zu ernsthaften Mißverständnissen kommt. Besonders sorgfältig wurden Erscheinungen behandelt, die bei Lernenden mit der Muttersprache Deutsch leicht zu Irrtümern führen können. Verständlicherweise konnten aus Platzgründen nicht sämtliche Probleme und Aspekte der englischen Grammatik aufgenommen werden, doch sind alle berücksichtigt, die in der ersten Phase des Fremdsprachenerwerbs auftauchen, also etwa im Bereich der Sekundarstufe I (5.–10. Schuljahr) an deutschen Schulen.

Das Buch enthält nicht nur grammatische Strukturen, sondern auch einige Kapitel zu den wichtigsten Redeabsichten, in denen gezeigt wird, wie man sich ausdrückt, um eine bestimmte Tatsache mitzuteilen (z.B. Erlaubnis oder Verpflichtung) oder um ein bestimmtes Verhalten beim Partner zu erzielen (z.B. eine Einladung oder Bitte aussprechen).

Der richtige Gebrauch der grammatischen Strukturen wird anhand von realistischen Beispielen und alltäglichen Situationen dargestellt. Die Beispielsätze zeigen nicht nur, wie eine bestimmte grammatische Struktur gebildet wird, sondern auch, wie man sie anwendet und was man damit aussagt. Die Beispielsätze stehen numeriert in den umrandeten Kästen, die wichtigen Wörter sind **farbig** oder **halbfett** hervorgehoben. Numerierung und Hervorhebung wiederholen sich in den Anmerkungen, was zur Einsicht in Sinn und Gebrauch der grammatischen Struktur beiträgt.

Die Anmerkungen sind in besonders einfachem Englisch geschrieben, so daß sie ohne große Mühe zu verstehen sind. Unnötige grammatische Fachausdrücke wurden vermieden. Die hauptsächlich benutzten Ausdrücke sind im Glossar (S. 159 und 160) erklärt. Inhaltsverzeichnis und Index (S. 154 ff.) erleichtern das Auffinden gesuchter Strukturen oder Redeabsichten. Wichtig sind auch die Verweise (▷), die sich in allen Kapiteln finden. Hat eine Struktur verschiedene Bedeutungen, die sich nicht alle in einem Abschnitt zusammenfassen lassen, so führt der Verweis zu anderen Bedeutungen oder Funktionen dieser Struktur. Durch die Verweise wird auch die Verbindung zwischen bestimmten grammatischen Strukturen und einzelnen Redeabsichten aufgezeigt.

Wie schon der Titel sagt, steht das gesprochene Englisch im Mittelpunkt, die meisten Beispiele entstammen der gesprochenen Sprache. Die geschriebene Sprache darf jedoch nicht vernachlässigt werden, weshalb auf Unterschiede im Gebrauch der geschriebenen und gesprochenen Sprache stets hingewiesen wird. Wo es wichtig ist, wird auch angegeben, ob ein bestimmter Sprachgebrauch mehr der formellen Sprache oder der informellen Umgangssprache angehört. Auf Unterschiede des amerikanischen und britischen Englisch wird in wichtigen Fällen aufmerksam gemacht.

1 Word order

1.1 SUBJECT AND VERB IN STATEMENTS

1 **Subject**	**Verb**		**(Direct object)**
a The girls	are working.		
b Susan	has got		a new job.
c She	earns		a lot of money.
2 **Subject**	**Verb**	**Complement**	
a Susan	is	very nice.	
b Susan and Kay	are	nice girls.	
3 **Subject**	**Verb**	**Adverb phrase**	
a Peter	is	in here.	
b The boys	are staying	at home.	

These sentences are statements. The word order in a statement is

1 subject + verb (+ direct object) or
2 subject + verb + complement or
3 subject + verb + adverb phrase ▷ 1.5

1.2 NEGATIVE STATEMENTS

Subject	**Auxiliary** or **modal verb + n't/not**	**(Verb)**	
a My pen	**isn't**		in my desk.
b I	**can't**	find	it.
c I	**don't**	know	where it is.
d John	**did not**	take	your pen.

In a negative statement an auxiliary or modal verb + **n't/not** comes after the subject.

▷ 5.8 (auxiliary verbs); 7.1 (modal verbs); 8.1

1.3 QUESTIONS

(Question word)	Auxiliary or modal verb	Subject	(Verb)	
Where	are	the girls?		
	Is	Ann	playing	tennis?
When	will	she	be	back?
	Did	David	go	with her?

In a question, an auxiliary or modal verb comes before the subject. But ▷ 21.2

▷ 5.8 (auxiliary verbs); 7.1 (modal verbs); 8.2; 8.3 (negative questions)

1.4 DIRECT AND INDIRECT OBJECTS

	Subject	Verb	Indirect object	Direct object
1	**Subject**	**Verb**	**Indirect object**	**Direct object**
	Mrs Fenton	gave	Jane	a record.
	She	sent	Peter	a book.
2	**Subject**	**Verb**	**Direct object**	**Indirect object**
	Mrs Fenton	gave	the record	to Jane.
	She	sent	the book	to Peter.

1 The indirect object without **to** comes before the direct object.

2 The indirect object with **to** comes after the direct object.

The **direct** object is the thing or person to which something happens. The **indirect** object is the person to whom somebody gives something.

▷ 18.3 (direct and indirect objects)

1.5 ADVERB PHRASES

(Adverb phrase)	Subject	Verb	(Direct object)	(Adverb phrase)
	The Smiths	eat		at seven.
	Pat	has	her lunch	in the kitchen.
At school	we	have	our lunch	at half past twelve.
In the evenings	we	watch	television.	

An adverb phrase can come either at the beginning or at the end of a statement.

The subject stays before the verb.

▷ 24.10 (place and time)

1.6 SUB CLAUSES WITH *WHEN, IF, BECAUSE* ETC

	(Sub clause)	Main clause	(Sub clause)
1	When it's nice, If we want to,	we go out. we take a picnic.	
2		We take a picnic I want to go home	if we want to. because it's raining.

A sub clause can come either

1 before the main clause or

2 after the main clause.

The main clause has the normal word order of subject + verb (+ object/complement/adverb phrase). ▷ 1.1

These sub clauses begin with a conjunction, e.g. *when, if, because, after.*

The word order after the conjunction is the same as in a main clause, e.g. *it's nice, we want to.*

▷ 27.1 (sub clauses, relative clauses and reported clauses)

2 Verbs: Talking about the present

2.1 THE PRESENT TENSE OF *BE*

I'**m** sorry. I'**m not** late; but **am** I too early? –
No, you **aren't**. You'**re** just in time for the party.

Peter'**s** here, but Ann **isn't**. **Is** she ill again? –
Yes, she **is**. And David'**s** ill, too. He'**s** at home in bed.

It'**s** a good party. – Yes, it **is**.

Billy and Sandy **are** from Glasgow. They'**re** on holiday here. –
Sandy and I **are** visiting John. We'**re** here for a week.

Form

I **am**	we **are**
you **are**	you **are**
he **is** she **is** it **is**	they **are**

Short forms

'm = am			
're = are		**aren't** = are not	
's = is		**isn't** = is not	

We use short forms in spoken English. ▷ 38.2

Short answers

Yes, I **am.**	No, I'**m not**.
Yes, you **are**.	No, you **aren't**.
Yes, he/she/it **is**.	No, he/she/it **isn't**.
Yes, we/you/they **are**.	No, we/you/they **aren't**.

▷ 20.1 (personal pronouns)

2.2 THE PRESENT TENSE OF *HAVE (GOT)*

1 **have got**

I'**ve got** a bicycle. **Have** you **got** a bicycle, too?
Yes, I **have**. And we'**ve got** a car.

Mr Fell'**s got** a Mini. **Has** Mr Jones **got** a car?
No, he **hasn't**. He **hasn't got** a car, but he'**s got** a motor-bike.

Have you **got** a motor-bike?
I **haven't got** a motor-bike, but my friend **has**.

2 **have**

Mr and Mrs Green **have** a swimming-pool in their garden.
This town **hasn't** a cinema.

Form

1 I'**ve got**	we'**ve got**
you'**ve got**	you'**ve got**
he'**s got**	they'**ve got**
she'**s got**	
it'**s got**	
2 I **have**	we **have**
you **have**	you **have**
he **has**	they **have**
she **has**	
it **has**	

Short forms

've	= have	**haven't**	= have not
's	= has	**hasn't**	= has not

Short answers

Yes, I/you **have**.	No, I/you **haven't**.
Yes, he/she/it **has**.	No, he/she/it **hasn't**.
Yes, we/you/they **have**.	No, we/you/they **haven't**.

Use

1 In speech we use **have got**.

2 In writing we often use **have**.

Here **have** and **have got** = **own** or **possess.** *(I've got a dog. It's* my *dog.)*

▷ 5.5 (other uses of *have*); 5.6 (USA)

2.3 THE PRESENT CONTINUOUS TENSE

1 Jane **is talking** to Susan. They**'re planning** their holiday.
2 They **aren't using** the living-room.
3 What **are** you **doing** now, John? **Are** you **writing** a letter?
4 No, I**'m not**. I'm making a shopping list.

Form

I'**m** talk**ing**	we'**re** talk**ing**
you'**re** talk**ing**	you'**re** talk**ing**
he'**s**/she'**s**/it'**s** talk**ing**	they'**re** talk**ing**

1 The present continuous tense is the present tense of **be** + the -ing form of a verb.
▷ 2.1 (*be*); 30.3,5,6 (spelling of the -ing form)
2 In the negative **n't/not** comes after a form of **be**.
3 In questions a form of **be** comes before the subject. But ▷ 21.2
4 We form short answers with a form of **be**.

Use We use the present continuous tense to talk about things that are happening **at the moment** *(now)*.

▷ 2.5; 4.4 (with a future meaning)

2.4 THE SIMPLE PRESENT TENSE

Positive sentences

1a We **sit** here every evening. I sometimes **read** a book.
b Mary **reads** the newspaper or **watches** television.

Form

I sit	we sit
you sit	you sit
he/she/it sits	they sit

1a With **I**, **you**, **we** and **they**, we use the basic form of the verb, e.g. *sit, read.*
b In the third person singular (e.g. with **he, she** or **it**), the verb ends in **-s** or **-es**, e.g. *reads, watches.* ▷ 30.1-3,6 (pronunciation and spelling).

A very few verbs have an irregular pronunciation in the third person singular, e.g. *does* [dʌz], *says* [sez]. ▷ 40

Negative sentences

2a I **don't live** in England; I live in Scotland.
b My friend **doesn't come** from France; he comes from Germany.

Form

I **don't** live you **don't** live he/she/it **doesn't** live	we **don't** live you **don't** live they **don't** live

2a With **I**, **you**, **we** and **they**, we form the negative with **don't** (= do not) and the basic form of the verb.

b In the third person singular we form the negative with **doesn't** (= does not) and the basic form of the verb (**without** -*s*), e.g. *live.*

Questions

3a **Do** you **like** this music? – Yes, it's nice.
b Which record **do** you **want**? – This one here.
c **Does** Jane **want** a record? – No.
d How **does** she **feel** now? – Better, she says.

Form

Do I like . . . ? **Do** you like . . . ? **Does** he/she/it like . . . ?	**Do** we like . . . ? **Do** you like . . . ? **Do** they like . . . ?

3a, b In questions with **I**, **you**, **we** and **they**, we put **do** before the subject.

c, d In questions in the third person singular we put **does** before the subject. We use the basic form of the verb (**without** -*s*), e.g. *like.*

For questions with *who* and *what* asking about the subject (e.g. *Who likes music?*) ▷ 21.2

Short answers

4a Do you think Peter's at the café? – Yes, I **do**.
b Does Ann know where it is? – No, she **doesn't**.

Form

Yes, I/you/we/they **do**. Yes, he/she/it **does**.	No, I/you/we/they **don't**. No, he/she/it **doesn't**.

Uses of the simple present tense

We use the simple present to talk about

1 things that happen **again and again**, e.g. *every evening, sometimes.*

2 **facts**, things that stay the same for a long time, e.g. *I live in Scotland.*

3 **feelings** e.g. *I like, I want*

4 **thoughts** e.g. *I think, I know*

▷ 2.5; 2.8 (dramatic use); 4.1 (in a sub clause of future time); 4.5 (with a future meaning); 11 (if-clauses)

2.5 PRESENT CONTINUOUS OR SIMPLE PRESENT? (A)

Present continuous	Simple present
1 Mary**'s listening** to the radio (now/at the moment).	2 She **listens** to the music programme (every day/sometimes).
3 Mr Brown **isn't working** this morning/today.	4 He **doesn't work** on Saturdays/at weekends.
	5 I **want** a cup of tea. I **think** there's a café near here.

Can + see/hear

6 I **can see** a café over there.

The present continuous and the simple present tenses do not have the same uses. Study carefully the differences between them:

	Present continuous		Simple present
1,3	things that are happening **at the moment/now**	2,4	things that happen **again and again**

5 We normally use the simple present, not the present continuous with these verbs: want, like, love, believe, think (= *believe*), understand, know, suppose, mean, remember, forget, have (= *possess*), belong, own, need, cost, seem.

6 We use **can** instead of a present tense with **see** and **hear.**

But ▷ 2.6,7,8; 28.7 (after *here* and *there*)

2.6 PRESENT CONTINUOUS OR SIMPLE PRESENT? (B)

Present continuous	Simple present
1 Mrs Haynes **is travelling** to work by bus *this week*. Her car is in the garage for repairs.	2 She *usually* **travels** by car.
3 **I'm learning** English at evening classes *this year.*	4 I **learn** English at school.

Remember that we use the present continuous tense for things that are happening at the moment and the simple present tense for things that happen again and again (▷ 2.5).
Then study this difference between the two tenses:

	Present continuous		Simple present
1,3	something that is happening again and again but only for **a short time**, e.g. *this week*	2,4	something that happens again and again over **a longer time**, e.g. *usually*

2.7 THE PRESENT CONTINUOUS TENSE WITH *ALWAYS*

I've forgotten my money. –	You**'re always forgetting** your money.
Can you pay for my coffee? –	But I**'m always paying** for your coffee.

Form ▷ 2.3
Always comes between **be** and the -ing form.

Use We use the present continuous tense with **always** to talk about something that happens **too often.**

▷ 24.11 (adverbs of frequency)

2.8 THE SIMPLE PRESENT TENSE: DRAMATIC USE

1 A car **stops** outside the National Bank. Three men **get** out and the driver **stays** in the car. The three men **walk** into the bank and **take** out their guns ...

2 Ellis **throws** the ball in to Snow, but he **loses** it. Watson **gives** the ball to Tanner. Tanner **goes** past two men, he **shoots**, but the ball **hits** a Liverpool player...

Form ▷ 2.4

Use We sometimes use the simple present tense
1 to tell a story, to describe the dramatic action of a play or film.
2 to describe actions (e.g. in sport) while they are happening.

3 Verbs: Talking about the past

3.1 THE PAST TENSE OF *BE*

I **was** at Pat's house last night. I **wasn't** at the club. –
Were you there all evening? – Yes, I **was**.

Philip **was** at the club yesterday. –
Was he with Susan? – No, he **wasn't**.

John and Jane **were** there, too. But they **weren't** there for long. –
Were the Jones sisters at Pat's house? – Yes, they **were**.

Form

I **was**	we **were**
you **were**	you **were**
he/she/it **was**	they **were**

Short forms

wasn't = was not
weren't = were not

Short answers

Yes, I/he/she/it **was**.	No, I/he/she/it **wasn't**.
Yes, you/we/they **were**.	No, you/we/they **weren't**.

3.2 THE PAST TENSE OF *HAVE (GOT)*

1 **have got**

I'**d got**/I'**d** a little money yesterday evening, but I **hadn't got**/I **hadn't** enough for a taxi. –
Had you **got**/**Had** you enough for the bus? – Yes, I **had**.

2 **have**

I **had** a little money yesterday evening, but I **didn't have** enough for a taxi. –
Did you **have** enough for the bus? – Yes, I **did**.

Form **'d got, 'd** or **had** in all persons.

Short forms	
'd	= had
hadn't	= had not

Short answers

1 Yes, I/you/he/we/they **had**. No, I/you/he/we/they **hadn't**.
2 Yes, I **did**. etc ▷ 3.3

1 We sometimes form negatives and questions with **had**.
2 We often form negatives and questions with **did**. ▷ 3.3; 5.6 (USA)

Use Here **had (got)** = **owned** or **possessed** (*I had a dog. It was* my *dog.*)

▷ 5.5 (uses of *have*)

3.3 THE SIMPLE PAST TENSE

Positive sentences

1 I **enjoyed** my holiday last week. I **liked** Brighton. I **wanted** to stay longer.
2 Our family **went** to Brighton two years ago. We **swam** in the sea every day.

Form 1 We form the simple past tense of most verbs with **-ed** or **-d**, e.g. *enjoyed, liked.*

▷ 30.3-6 (pronunciation and spelling)

2 Some verbs have an irregular past form, e.g. *went, swam.* ▷ 40
Regular and irregular past forms are the same in all persons (but not **be** ▷ 3.1).

Negative sentences

It was a long journey yesterday. We **didn't start** very early, and we **didn't get** home until nine o'clock.

Form We form the negative with **didn't** (= did not) and the basic form of the verb (**without** *-ed*), e.g. *start.*

Questions

Did Nora **enjoy** the holiday? – Yes, she **did**.
Did she **swim** in the sea? – No, she **didn't**.
What time **did** you **arrive** home? – Nine o'clock.

Form We form questions with **did** and the basic form of the verb (**without** *-ed*), e.g. *enjoy*.
For questions with *who* and *what* asking about the subject (e.g. *Who enjoyed the holiday?*) ▷ 21.2

Short answers	
Yes, I/you/he/we/they **did**.	No, I/you/he/we/they **didn't**.

Use of the simple past

We use the simple past tense to talk about things that happened at a time that is now finished, e.g. *last week, two years ago, yesterday.*
We often use the simple past tense to tell a story.

▷ 3.5 (present perfect or simple past)

3.4 THE PRESENT PERFECT TENSE

1 **I've cleaned** my shoes. (So they're clean now.)
2 Mr Green **has bought** a new car. (So it's his car now.)
3 Sally **hasn't eaten** any toast. (The toast is still on the table.)
4a **Have** you **finished** your homework?
b No, I **haven't**. I'm still doing it.

Form

I/you **have cleaned**
he/she/it **has cleaned**
we/you/they **have cleaned**

1 The present perfect tense is the present tense of **have** + the -ed form (past participle).
▷ 2.2 (*have*); 30.3-6 (pronunciation and spelling of the -ed form)

2 Some verbs have an irregular past participle, e.g. *bought*. ▷ 40

3 In the negative, **n't/not** comes after **have** or **has**.

4 a In questions, **have** or **has** comes before the subject. But ▷ 21.2
b We form short answers with **have/has**.

5 I've just written that letter.

6a You haven't posted the letter yet .
b Have you found those stamps yet ? – No, not yet.

7a Have you seen Sarah today ?
b No, I haven't. I haven't seen her this week .

8a How long has Ann lived here?
b Oh, only for six months. She's been here since April.

9a Have you ever eaten rabbit? – Yes, lots of times.
b Well, I've never had it.

Form Note the irregular past participles of **be** and **have**.

8b	**be**	–	**have been**
9b	**have**	–	**have had**

Use We use the present perfect tense to talk about

1-4 the present result of a past action.
5 something that happened only a short time ago, e.g. *just*.
6 an action that we are waiting for, e.g. *yet*.
7 something that happened during a time that is not yet finished, e.g. *today, this week*.
8 something that began in the past and has stayed the same up to the present, e.g. for *six months*, since *April*.
9 something that happened during a time which began in the past and has gone on up to the present, e.g. *ever, never*.

NOTE In British English we sometimes use the present perfect tense where Americans use the simple past, e.g. *Did you find those stamps yet?* (6b).

▷ 3.5; 5.4 (*been to* and *gone to*)

3.5 PRESENT PERFECT OR SIMPLE PAST?

	Present perfect	Simple past
1	They**'ve opened** the new road. (So it's open now.)	Yes, they **opened** it *last week*.
2	**I've** *just* **got** up.	Peter **got** up *at half past six*.
3	I **haven't seen** this new film 'Cowboy Joe' *yet*.	Tom **saw** it in town *on Saturday*.
4	It **hasn't rained** *today*.	And it **didn't rain** *yesterday*.
5	*How long* **has** Mrs Peters **had** that car?	Let me see. *When* **did** she **buy** it?
6	**Have** you *ever* **travelled** by plane?	Yes, we **travelled** to London by plane *six months ago*.

The present perfect and simple past tenses do not have the same uses. Study carefully the differences between them:

	Present perfect	Simple past
1	the present result of a past action	a past action
2	a short time ago	a longer time ago
3	something that we are waiting for	something that is already over
4	an unfinished time	a finished time
5	something that has stayed the same	something that happened
6	a time up to the present	a time in the past

We use the **simple past** (not the present perfect) with a phrase of past time which says (or asks) when something happened, e.g.

1 *last week*	3 *on Saturday*	5 *When . . . ?*
2 *at half past six*	4 *yesterday*	6 *six months ago*

3.6 THE PAST PERFECT TENSE

Remember:

Present perfect

1 Alan's got no money. He's *spent* it all.

Past perfect

2a Alan had no money last Sunday. He**'d spent** it all.

b I didn't go to see the film last night because I**'d seen** it before.

c **Had** Mrs Williams already **arrived** when you got to the station? – No, she **hadn't**.

d After we **had looked** round the museum, we went to a restaurant.

3 We looked round the museum, and then we went to a restaurant.

Form **Had** + the -ed form (past participle).

Short forms	**'d** = had	**hadn't** = had not

Some past participles end in **-ed**, and some are irregular. ▷ 40
We form short answers with **had**. ▷ 3.2

Use

1 Remember that we use the **present** perfect tense to talk about the present result of a past action.

2 When we talk about the past, we sometimes talk about one thing that happened before another. We use the **past** perfect tense for the thing that happened **first** and the simple past tense for what happened **later**.

3 When one thing happened and then another, we can also use the simple past tense for both actions.

3.7 THE PAST CONTINUOUS TENSE

Remember:

Present continuous

1a What are you doing?
b I'*m waiting* for a bus.

Past continuous

2a What **were** you **doing** at six o'clock yesterday evening?
b At six o clock I was **waiting** for a bus.

3a And what **were** you **doing** when the policeman came? **Were** you **watching** television?
b Yes, I **was**. I **was watching** the news when he knocked at the door.

4 David telephoned while you **were talking** to Mrs Thurston.

Form **Was/were** (▷ 3.1) + the -ing form

We form short answers with **was/were**. ▷ 3.1

Use 1 Remember that we use the **present** continuous tense to talk about things that are happening **now**.

2 We use the **past** continuous tense to talk about things happening at a time in the past, e.g. *at six o'clock yesterday evening.*

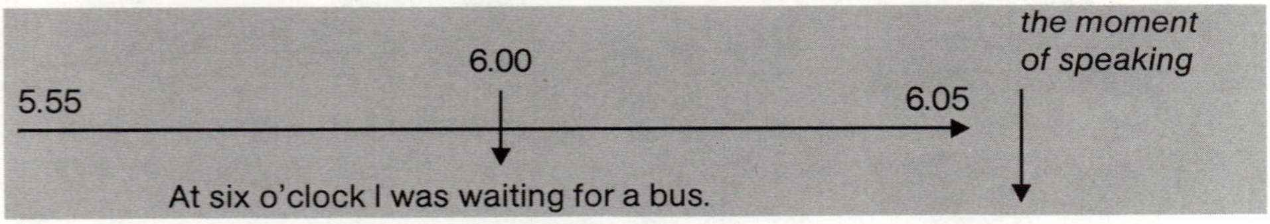

3,4 When we talk about the past, we sometimes talk about one thing that happened at the same time as another. If one action was going on for some time (e.g. *I was watching the news*), and a new action happened (e.g. *he knocked at the door*), we use the past continuous tense for the longer action.

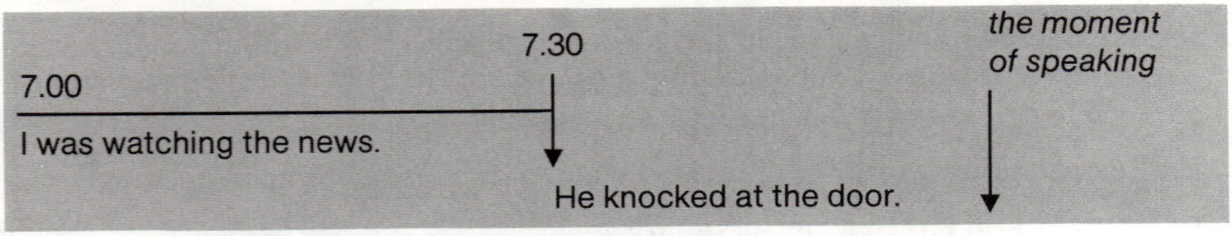

3.8 THE PRESENT PERFECT CONTINUOUS TENSE

1a Peter **has been working** in the garden since this morning, and he's still hard at work.
b How long **has** he **been digging**? – Oh, for hours.

2a Eric, you**'ve been reading** that book all day.
b Yes, I **have**, but I haven't finished it yet.

3a What **have** you **been doing** this afternoon, Alice?
b I**'ve been talking** to some friends at the club.

Form **Have been/has been** + the -ing form.

We form short answers with **have/has**. ▷ 2.2

Use 1 The present perfect continuous tense shows that an action began in the past and has gone on for some time.
We often use the tense in a question with *How long...?* or with *for* or *since* (▷ 25.7).

2 We can use the tense to talk about an action that is still happening.

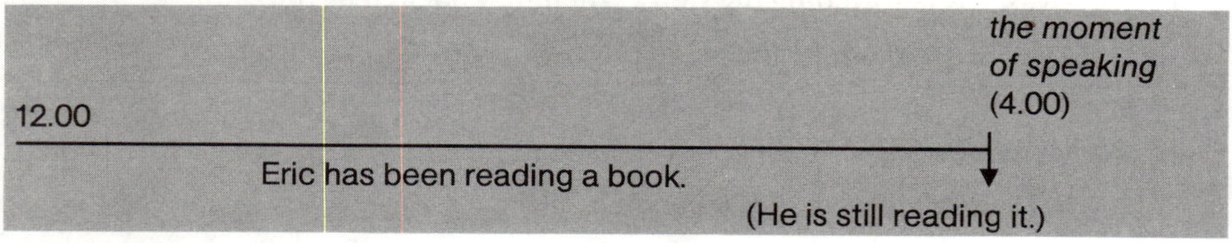

3 We can use the tense to talk about an action that finished a short time ago.

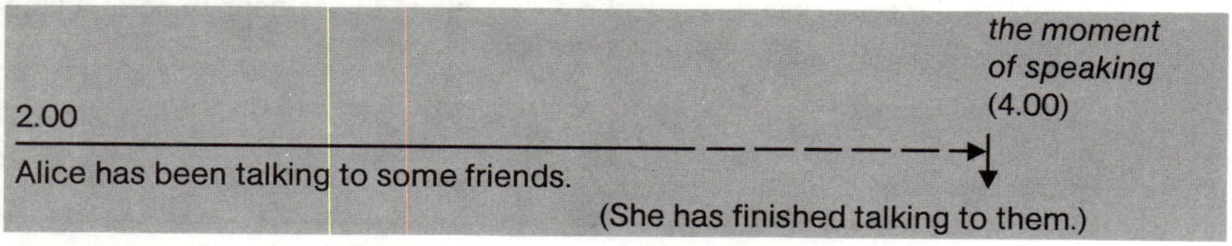

3.9 PRESENT PERFECT OR PRESENT PERFECT CONTINUOUS?

1a I'm pleased because **I've cut** the grass. (The grass is short now.)
b I'm tired because **I've been cutting** the grass. (The cutting went on for some time.)

2a **I've owned** this bicycle since I was fifteen. (something staying the same)
b **I've been riding** this bicycle since I was fifteen. (something happening)

3a Mrs Dobson **has lived** in Bristol for twenty years and **has worked** at the bookshop for ten years.
b Mrs Dobson **has been living** in Bristol for twenty years and **has been working** at the bookshop for ten years.

The present perfect and present perfect continuous tenses do not have the same uses. Study carefully the differences between them.

1 We use both tenses to talk about an action that finished a short time ago. We use the present perfect to talk about the present **result** of an action, and we use the present perfect continuous to show that an action has gone on **for some time**.

2 We use both tenses to talk about things that began in the past and have gone on up to the present. We use the present perfect to talk about something **staying the same** and the present perfect continuous to talk about something **happening**.

3 We can talk about some things either as **staying the same** (a) or as **happening** (b).

3.10 THE PAST PERFECT CONTINUOUS TENSE

Remember:

Present perfect continuous

1 We*'ve been cleaning* the house all afternoon, and we're going to have a cup of tea now.

Past perfect continuous

2 Mrs Croft felt very tired yesterday afternoon because she **had been working** hard since seven o'clock.

3 How long **had** you **been waiting** when the Browns arrived?

4 **Had** Keith **been driving** a lorry before he got the job at the factory last year? – Yes, he **had**. He**'d been working** as a driver for three years.

Form **Had been** + the -ing form.

We form short answers with **had**. ▷ 3.2

Use 1 Remember that we use the **present** perfect continuous tense (▷ 3.8) to talk about an action that has gone on up to the **present** time.

2-4 We use the **past** perfect continuous tense to talk about an action that went on up to a time **in the past**.

2

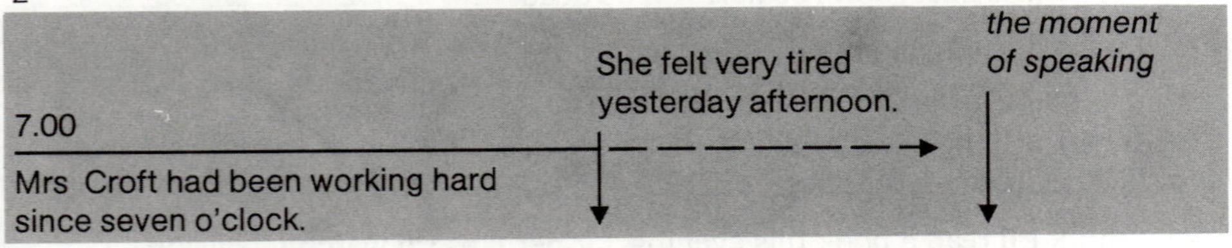

3

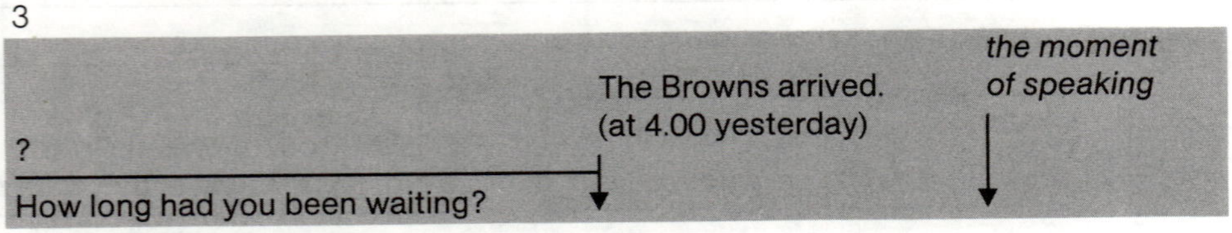

3.11 *USED TO*

1 I **used to** swim in the river when I was a boy.

2 **Did** you **use to** do it very often? – Yes, I **did**. I used to go there every weekend.

3a The water **didn't use to** be so dirty in those days.
b The water **used not to** be so dirty in those days.
c The water **never used to** be so dirty in those days.

4 Nobody swims there now.

Form 1 **Used to** + the basic form of the verb in all persons

2 We form questions and short answers with **did**.

3 The negative is
a usually **didn't use to**
b sometimes **used not to** or
c **never used to** (more emphatic)

Use 1-3 **Used to** means that something often happened in the past but does not happen now.

4 There is no present tense of **used to**. We use the simple present tense to talk about things that often happen these days.

▷ 7.11 (habits: *will* and *would*); 15.4 (*be used to*)

4 Verbs: Talking about the future

4.1 *WILL*

1a Life **will** be very different in 100 years' time.
b Yes, it **will**, but I **won't** be here. I**'ll** be dead.

2a I think Birmingham **will** win on Saturday.
b No, they **won't**. They **won't** beat Leeds.

3a When **will** the party begin?
b It**'ll** begin when the guests arrive.

4 I think I**'ll** read a book this evening. Or perhaps I**'ll** watch television.

Form **Will** in all persons.

Short forms

'll = will **won't** = will not

Short answers

Yes, I/you/he/we/they **will**.
No, I/you/he/we/they **won't**.

Use 1 We use **will** to talk about something in the future (often a long way in the future). It does **not** mean that somebody **has decided** on an action.

2 We use **will** to talk about things which the speaker cannot control. (We use it to make predictions. ▷ 33.6)

3 If we use **will** in the main clause, we use the simple present tense in a sub clause of future time, e.g. *when the guests arrive.* ▷ 11 (if-clauses); 13.1

4 If we are talking about things that we have not yet decided to do or that we are deciding to do at the moment of speaking, we can use **will**. ▷ 4.3

▷ 4.3; 4.6 (the future continuous; 4.9 (the future perfect); 4.10 (uses of *will* and *shall*)

4.2 BE GOING TO

1 We**'re going to** walk over the hills this afternoon. –
Are you **going to** take a picnic? – Yes, we **are**.

2 Look at those black clouds up there. It**'s going to** rain.
It **isn't going to** be nice enough for a picnic.

Use 1 We use **going to** to talk about things people have **decided** to do in the future.

▷ 34.3 (Communication: intentions)

2 We also use **going to** to talk about the future when there is something in the present (e.g. *black clouds*) which tells us about the future (often the near future).

▷33.6 (Communication: predictions)

4.3 WILL OR BE GOING TO?

Will	Be going to
1 Trains **will** be much faster in the future.	3 That boat's full of water. Look: It**'s going to** sink!
2 Do you want a newspaper? – Yes, I think I**'ll** buy 'The Sun' today.	4 I**'m going to** read 'Star Wars'. I bought the book last week.

Will and **be going to** do not have the same uses. Study carefully the differences between them.

We use **will**

1 to talk about things in the future which we **cannot control** (**not** things that we **have decided** to do).
2 when we **are deciding** to do something **at the moment of speaking.**

We use **be going to**

3 when there is **something in the present** which tells us about the future.
4 to talk about things we have **already decided** to do.

4.4 THE PRESENT CONTINUOUS TENSE WITH A FUTURE MEANING

Are you **doing** anything tonight? –
Yes, I**'m playing** tennis. We've got a game against another club.

Are you **taking** a holiday this year? –
Yes, we've just arranged a holiday. We**'re spending** ten days in Spain.

Form ▷ 2.3

Use We often use the present continuous tense to talk about things that people have **arranged** to do in the future.

This meaning is almost the same as **be going to** used for things people have decided to do (▷ 4.3).

4.5 THE SIMPLE PRESENT TENSE WITH A FUTURE MEANING

What time **does** your plane **go**? –
It **leaves** at half past ten on Saturday, and we **arrive** in Rome at twelve o'clock.

Form ▷ 2.4

Use We sometimes use the simple present tense to talk about a **programme** or **timetable** in the future.

4.6 THE FUTURE CONTINUOUS TENSE

1a Mr Briggs is 65, so he **will be leaving** the company next month.
b **Will** you **be staying** late at the office tomorrow? –
Yes, I **will**. I've a lot of work to do.

2a I've got all the garden to dig – I**'ll be doing** it all day.
b We're washing-up now, but next week we **won't be washing** up – we**'ll be lying** on the beach in the sun!

Form **Will** (▷ 4.1) **+ be** + the -ing form.

Use 1 We use the future continuous tense to talk about things which are **fairly certain** to happen in the future.

This meaning is almost the same as the present continuous tense with a future meaning. ▷ 4.4

2 We also use the future continuous to talk about actions that will be **going on** at a time in the future.

4.7 *BE TO*

The American President **is to** visit Russia later this year.

The two leaders **are to** meet in Moscow.

When **is** the Minister for Industry **to** open the new factory?

Use We use **be to** to talk about something that has been officially arranged to take place in the future.

We use **be to** mostly in formal written English.

▷ 34.1 (*be to* used for orders)

4.8 *BE ABOUT TO*

I'm **about to** leave for the station. The train leaves in twenty minutes. –
I think it's just **about to** start raining. –
Yes, it **is**. I'd better put my coat on.

Use We use **be about to** to talk about things which are going to happen in the very near future.

4.9 THE FUTURE PERFECT TENSE

1a Let's go out tonight.
b All right. I have some work to do, but I'**ll have finished** it by about eight.

2a Can I have the book back tomorrow, please? **Will** you **have read** it by then?
b No, I **won't**. I **won't have read** it until the weekend.

Form **Will** (▷ 4.1) **+ have** + the -ed form.

Use We use the future perfect tense to talk about something that will be **completed** at a time in the future.
We often use the tense with *finish*.
We often use *by* and (in negative sentences) *till/until*. ▷ 25.5

4.10 USES OF *WILL* AND *SHALL*

Will		
Future	Fiona **will** be 16 next month.	▷ 4.1
Certainty	I sent the parcel last week, so they'**ll** have it by now.	▷ 7.9
Habits	Our cat loves television. She'**ll** usually watch it all day.	▷ 7.11
Formal orders	All pupils **will** be in school at nine o'clock.	▷ 34.1
Requests	**Will** you shut the window, please?	▷ 34.2
Promises	I'**ll** give you back your money soon, I promise.	▷ 34.10
Offering	I'**ll** carry your bags for you.	▷ 34.11
Refusing	The car **won't** start. What's wrong with it?	▷ 34.11
Invitations	**Will** you/**Won't** you sit down?	▷ 34.12
Shall		
Formal orders	All books **shall** be returned to the library.	▷ 34.1
Suggestions	**Shall** we go out this evening?	▷ 34.4
Promises	You **shall** go to the zoo, I promise. I **shall** take you on Saturday.	▷ 34.10
Offering	**Shall** I carry your bags for you?	▷ 34.11

▷ 7.12 (uses of *would* and *should*)

4.11 PAST PLANS: *WAS/WERE GOING TO*

What did you do at the weekend? –
Well, we **were going to** walk over the hills, but it rained, so we stayed at home.

Use We use **was/were going to** to talk about a past plan – a plan that somebody changed or gave up.

5 Verbs: *be, have* and *do*

5.1 AUXILIARY VERBS (HELPING VERBS)

Philip **is** playing tennis.
Debbie **has** gone to a football match.
I **don't** like sport.

We use **be, have** and **do** as auxiliary verbs. Auxiliary verbs help to form tenses.

▷ 5.2 *(be)*; 5.5 *(have)*; 5.7 *(do)*; 5.8

5.2 USES OF *BE*

1 Jane **is** ill. She **wasn't** at school today. She**'s been** in bed since last night.
2 She **wasn't feeling** very well yesterday, but she**'s eating** a little now.
3 This medicine **is** best **taken** after meals. It must **be taken** three times a day.

Use We use **be**

1 as a verb with a complement or adverb phrase ▷ 2.1; 3.1
2 as an auxiliary verb (helping verb) in continuous tenses ▷ 2.3; 3.7, 8,10; 7.14
3 as an auxiliary verb in the passive ▷ 10

▷ 4.7; 34.1 *(be to)*

5.3 *IT + BE* AND *THERE + BE*

Present

1 **It's** half past twelve. – Yes, **it is**.
(= The time is half past twelve.)

2 **There's** no time for a meal. – No, **there isn't**.
(= No time exists . . ./We have no time . . .)

Past

1 **It wasn't** expensive to go to London.
(= The fare wasn't expensive.)

2 But **there weren't** any trains on Sundays.
(= Trains didn't go on Sundays.)

Present perfect

1 **Has it been** very wet here? – Yes, **it has**.
(= Has the weather been very wet?)

2 **Has there been** a storm? – Yes, **there has**.
(= Has a storm happened?)

1 **it + be**

Form After **it** the verb is always singular, e.g. *it's*.

Use We use **it** instead of a noun phrase, e.g. *the time, the fare, the weather.*

▷ 20.2 (uses of *it*)

2 **there + be**

Form If the noun after **there + be** is plural, then the verb is plural too, e.g. *there* weren't *any trains.*

Use We use **there + be** to say that something exists.

After **there + be** we use a noun phrase, e.g. *no time, any trains, a storm,* but not a noun with **the**.

▷ 28.7 (emphatic use of *there*)

5.4 *BEEN TO* AND *GONE TO*

1 Have you ever **been to** America?
Yes, I went to New York two years ago.

2 Is Judy in America?
Yes, she's **gone to** Los Angeles. She'll be back next week.

We sometimes use the past participle of **be (been)** instead of the past participle of **go (gone).**

1 **Been to** = gone somewhere and now come back
2 **Gone to** = gone somewhere and still there

5.5 USES OF *HAVE*

Auxiliary verb

1 **Have** you **sold** your car? – Yes, it **had done** 100,000 miles.

Have (got)

2 You **had** a car last year. – Yes, but we **haven't got** one now.

Have (got) to

3 **Have** you **got to** walk to school now? –
It's too far. I **have to** go by bus.

Full verb

4 I**'m having** a sandwich. What about you? –
I think I**'ll** just **have** a cup of tea.

5 **Are** you **having** a good holiday? –
Yes, we**'ve had** some lovely weather, haven't we?

6 Did you **have a look** at our new car? –
Yes, but I **didn't have a ride** in it.

Use

1 **Have** as an auxiliary verb (helping verb) in perfect tenses ▷ 3.4,6,8,10; 4.9; 5.1; 7.15

2 **Have (got)** meaning **own** or **possess** ▷ 2.2; 3.2; 5.6

3 **Have (got) to** meaning the same as **must** ▷ 7.4

Have as a full verb with other meanings, e.g.

4 **eat** or **drink** ▷ 34.11 (Communication: offering food and drink)

5 something **happening** to us

6 **have a look** = look (verb); **have a ride** = ride (verb) etc.

NOTE The full verb **have** can have a continuous form *(Are you having . . . ?)* and we form questions and negatives with **do** *(Did you have . . . ?)*.

▷ 10.8 *(have something done)*

5.6 *HAVE* IN AMERICAN ENGLISH

1 GB: **Have** you **got** a ticket to London? –
Yes, I **have**. But my friend **hasn't got** one.

2 USA: **Do** you **have** a ticket to New York? –
Yes, I **do**. But my friend **doesn't have** one.

1 **Have got** is more usual in British English (but we often use the full verb **have** in the past tense ▷ 3.2).

2 **Have** is more usual in American English. Questions, negatives and short answers are with **do**.

▷ 7.4 *(have [got] to)*

5.7 USES OF *DO*

Auxiliary verb

1a What **does** this word mean? – I **don't** know.
b **Did** you learn English at school? – Yes, I **did**.
2 **Don't** shout. I can hear you.

Full verb

3 What do you **do** in your free time?
What are you **doing** now?
I **did** something interesting yesterday.
What did you **do**?
4 I'm **doing** my homework. I've just **done** this exercise.

Use

1 As an auxiliary verb (helping verb) in the simple present and simple past tenses ▷ 2.4; 3.3
We use **do** in questions, negatives and short answers. And ▷ 5.8
2 As an auxiliary verb with the negative imperative. And ▷ 6.1

3 As a full verb, to talk about an action when we do not know or do not say what the action is.
4 As a full verb meaning e.g. *work at, finish*.

NOTE We use the auxiliary verb **do** with the full verb **do** in the simple present and simple past tenses, e.g. *What* do *you do? What* did *you do?*

5.8 USES OF THE AUXILIARY VERBS (*BE, HAVE* AND *DO*)

1 **I'm** writing a letter. **I've** almost finished.
2 **I'm not** writing to Debbie. She **hasn't** answered my last letter. And she **didn't** come to our last party.
3 **Are you** writing to your sister? **Have you** asked her to the party? **Does she** like parties?

4a	Alice is coming, **isn't** she?	She likes parties, **doesn't** she?
b	Yes, she **is**.	Yes, she **does**.
c	Peter hasn't answered, and John **hasn't** either.	He **didn't** last time.
d	John and Sally *are* coming, I know.	Yes, they *do* want to come.

1 In positive statements we use **be** and **have** to form tenses.

NOTE In two tenses only – the simple present and the simple past – we do not use an auxiliary.

2 In the negative we use **be**, **have** or **do** (or a modal verb ▷ 7.1) **+ n't/not**. ▷ 8.1
3 In questions we use **be**, **have** or **do** (or a modal verb) before the subject. ▷ 8.2
4 We also use an auxiliary verb (or modal verb)
a in question tags ▷ 8.5
b in short answers ▷ 8.4
c in short additions to statements ▷ 9.1
d in the emphatic form ▷ 28.6

6 The imperative and *let's*

6.1 THE IMPERATIVE

1 **Come** here, please, David.

2 **Help** me with this desk, you two.

3 **Don't drop** it.

4 **Do be** careful.

5a Thank you very much. **Have** a cup of tea now.
b No, thank you. But **you have** one.

6 **Go** straight ahead here and then **turn** right at the crossroads.

Form
1 The imperative is the basic form of the verb.
2 We use the same form to talk to two or more people.
3 We use **don't** in the negative.
4 We use **do** for emphasis. ▷ 28.6
5b We sometimes use **you** before the imperative.

Use We use the imperative
1,2 to give orders ▷ 34.1 (Communication)
3,4 to give warnings ▷ 34.6 (Communication)
5 for informal offers or invitations ▷ 34.11, 12 (Communication)
6 to tell someone how to do something

▷ 8.5 (question tags); 12.6 (reporting orders); 37.1 (punctuation)

6.2 *LET'S*

1 **Let's** sit down for a minute.

2 Oh, **don't let's** stop now./**let's not** stop now.

3 **Do let's** finish the work first.

Form
1 After **let's** we use the basic form of the verb.
2 We use **don't let's** or **let's not** in the negative.
3 We use **do** for emphasis ▷ 28.6

Use We use **let's** to make suggestions. ▷ 34.4 (Communication)

▷ 8.5 (question tags), 34.11 (*let me*)

7 Modal verbs

7.1 THE FORM AND USE OF MODAL VERBS

1a We **can** find the way all right.
b But I **must** look at the map.
c It **may** be in the car.

2a **Can you** drive a car? –
I **could** drive when I was 17.
b **Will it** start? –
No, and it **wouldn't** start yesterday either.

3a I **can't** repair cars. –
But you said yesterday you **could** repair them.
b The battery **may not** be very good. –
I thought yesterday it **might** be an old one.

4a We **could** walk, **couldn't** we?
b It **might** start now. –
Yes, it **might**.
c A taxi **would** be expensive. –
A bus **wouldn't**.
d A taxi will be quicker. I think we *should* take a taxi.

5a I've got £5. I'**ll be able to** pay for a taxi.
b Last year I **was allowed to** use my father's car.
c I'**ll have to** telephone a garage tomorrow.

Form 1 The modal verbs are

can, could, may, might, will, would, shall, should, ought to, must, need and **dare.**

A modal verb always has the same form. There is no **-s** ending, no **-ing** form and no **-ed** form. But ▷ 7.13 (*dare*)

After a modal verb we use the infinitive without **to** (▷ 14.1), e.g. *find, look, be.*

2 Modal verbs (and auxiliary verbs ▷ 5.8) come before the subject in questions.

3 Modal verbs (and auxiliary verbs) have **n't** or **not** after them in the negative.

4 We also use a modal verb (or auxiliary verb)

a in question tags ▷ 8.5
b in short answers ▷ 8.4
c in short additions to statements ▷ 9.1
d in the emphatic form ▷ 28.6

Present, past and future

2 The past forms of **can** and **will** are **could** and **would**.

3 In reported speech **can, may, will** and **shall** change to **could, might, would** and **should**. ▷ 12.3

4 But **could, might, would** and **should** also have their own meanings. We use them to talk about the present and the future too.

5 To talk about ability, permission and necessity in the past or the future, we can use **be able to, be allowed to** and **have (got) to**. ▷ 7.16

Use 1 We use modal verbs to talk about, for example,

a someone's ability to do an action ▷ 7.2
b if an action is necessary ▷ 7.4
c if an action is probable ▷ 7.7

We do not use modal verbs to say that something happens or something happened.

7.2 ABILITY: *CAN, COULD, BE ABLE TO*

1 I **can** swim. I **could** swim when I was five years old.
Jim **can't** swim yet, but he'**ll be able to** swim soon.
Can your sister swim? – Yes, she **can**.

2 When the children fell into the water, luckily they **were able to** hold on to the boat.
We weren't too far from land, so I **was able to** swim back and get help.

3 **Could** the children get back in the boat after they fell in? – No, they **couldn't**.
Were the children **able to** get back in the boat after they fell in? – No, they **weren't**.

4 We **could see** someone in the water, and we **could hear** shouting.

Form

	Positive	Negative
Present:	can am/are/is able to	can't/cannot am not/aren't/isn't able to
Past:	could was/were able to	couldn't/could not wasn't/weren't able to
Future:	will be able to	won't be able to

Short answers with can *and* could

Yes, I/you/he/we/they **can**.	Yes, I/you/he/we/they **could**.
No, I/you/he/we/they **can't**.	No, I/you/he/we/they **couldn't**.

Use

1 We use **can** and **could** to talk about ability. *I can swim* means that I am a swimmer, but it does not say how often I swim or if I am swimming now.

2 We use **was/were able to** to talk about ability + action. *I was able to swim back* means that I really did swim back.
We do **not** use **could** to talk about past actions which really happened.

3 We can use both **could** and **was/were able to** in questions and negative sentences.

4 We can use **can** and **could** with verbs of perception, e.g. *see, hear.* (**Could see** = saw) ▷ 2.5

▷ 7.8 (possibility: *could*); 7.16 (*be able to*)

7.3 PERMISSION: *CAN, MAY, BE ALLOWED TO*

1a People over 16 **can** drive/**may** drive/**are allowed to** drive a car in Britain.
People under 17 **can't** drive/**may not** drive/**aren't allowed to** drive a car.
My brother is 16; he**'ll be allowed to** drive a car soon.

b **Were** the pupils **allowed to** have their party at school last week? –
Yes, they **were**; but they **weren't allowed to** go on after midnight.

2a **Can** I use your bicycle, please, Jane? –
Yes, all right./Of course you can./I'm sorry, I need it myself.

b **May** I use your telephone, please, Mr Taylor? –
Yes. of course./Certainly you may./I'm afraid it's out of order.

c **Do you mind if** I use your telephone?

Form

	Positive	Negative
Present:	**can** **may** **am/are/is allowed to**	**can't/cannot** **may not** **am not/aren't/isn't allowed to**
Past:	**was/were allowed to**	**wasn't/weren't allowed to**
Future:	**will be allowed to**	**won't be allowed to**

We use short answers with **can/can't** (▷ 7.2) and with **may** for permission (▷ 7.7).

Use

1 We use **can, may** and **be allowed to** (▷ 7.16) to talk about permission. **May** is rather formal.

2a In informal English we use **can** to ask permission.

b In more formal English we use **may** to ask permission. **May** is more polite than **can**.

c We can also use **Do you mind if...?** to ask permission.

7.4 NECESSITY: *MUST, HAVE (GOT) TO, NEEDN'T, MUSTN'T*

Necessity

1 Teacher:
I'm going to buy your tickets tomorrow. You **must** bring the money tomorrow.

Pupils:
We**'ve got to** bring/We **have to** bring the money tomorrow.
We **had to** pay for the tickets last year too.
We**'ll have to** ask our parents for the money.

No necessity

2 **Have** we **got to** bring/**Do** we **have to** bring a letter from our parents? –
No, you **haven't got to** bring/you **don't have to** bring a letter.
We **didn't have to** bring a letter last year.

3 You **needn't** pay for your dinner. The school will pay.

Not allowed

4 Remember to bring the money for the tickets. You **mustn't** forget.
You **mustn't** play your radio during the lesson.

Form

	Positive	Negative
Present:		**needn't/need not**
	must	**mustn't/must not** ▷ 7.5
	have/has to	**don't/doesn't have to**
	have/has got to	**haven't/hasn't got to**
Past:	**had to**	**didn't have to**
Future:	**will have to**	**won't have to**
		won't need to

Short answers with must, needn't *and* mustn't

	No, I/you/he/we/they **needn't**.
Yes, I/you/he/we/they **must**.	No, I/you/he/we/they **mustn't**. ▷ 7.5

Use

1 **Necessity** means that you cannot get away from doing something. *You must buy a ticket* = You cannot go without a ticket.

We use **must** and **have (got) to** to talk about necessity. **Must** expresses the authority of the speaker, and **have (got) to** (▷ 7.16) expresses the authority of another person.

▷ 34.1 (Communication: orders)

2 We use the negative forms of **have (got) to** when there is **no necessity**.

3 We can also use **needn't** when there is **no necessity**.

NOTE We also use the full verb **need to**, e.g. *Do we need to pay for our dinner? We didn't need to pay for it last year.* The modal verb and the full verb have the same meaning.

4 We use **mustn't** when we are **not allowed** to do something.
You mustn't forget. = Don't forget.

7.5 *NEEDN'T* OR *MUSTN'T*?

1a The car's clean. I **needn't** wash it this week.
b It isn't raining. You **needn't** take a coat, but you can if you like.

2a The baby's asleep. We **mustn't** make a noise.
b Your father's very ill. He **mustn't** get up.

Needn't and **mustn't** have different meanings. It is important to know the difference between them, or there can be misunderstandings.

1 We use **needn't** when there is **no need** (= no necessity) to do something, but we can do it if we want to.

2 We use **mustn't** when we are **not allowed** to do something.

7.6 OBLIGATION: *OUGHT TO, SHOULD*

You're not fit. You **ought to** walk more. –
Yes, I know I **should** walk more.

You **oughtn't to** eat so much. –
I **shouldn't** have so many cakes, I know.

Ought I **to** see the doctor? **Should** I talk to him? –
Yes, you **ought (to)**. I think you **should**.

Form

Positive	Negative
ought to	oughtn't to/ought not to
should	shouldn't/should not

Short answers

Yes, I/you/he/we/they **ought (to)**.
No, I/you/he/we/they **oughtn't (to)**.

Yes, I/you/he/we/they **should**.
No, I/you/he/we/they **shouldn't**.

Use **Obligation** means that something is the right thing to do. *You ought to walk* = Walking is the right thing to do.

We use **ought to** and **should** to express obligation or to give advice. ▷ 34.5 (Communication)

There is little difference between **ought to** and **should**, but **ought to** is sometimes a little stronger than **should**.

▷ 7.12 (other uses of *should*); 36.1,2 (Communication: disapproving and blaming someone)

7.7 PROBABILITY: *MAY, MIGHT*

1 Your friends haven't come. They **may** be/**might** be at the club. – Yes, perhaps they're at the club.

2 They **may not**/**might not** come this evening. – Yes, perhaps they won't come this evening.

3 **Do you think** they'**ll** come on the next bus? – Yes, they **may**/**might**.

Form

Positive	Negative
may	may not
might	might not/mightn't

Short answers

Yes, I/you/he/we/they **may**.
No, I/you/he/we/they **may not**.

Yes, I/you/he/we/they **might**.
No, I/you/he/we/they **might not**/**mightn't**.

Use We use **may** and **might** to talk about

1 probability in the present.

2 probability in the future. ▷ 7.14 (+ *be* + -ing form); 7.15 (probability in the past)

There is little difference between **may** and **might**, but a speaker who uses **might** is less sure.

3 To ask questions, we use **Do you think...?** and **will**.

▷ 33.4 (Communication: being sure and unsure)

7.8 POSSIBILITY: *COULD*

It's a nice day. We **could** go down to the beach. –
I **couldn't** sit on the beach for long in this hot sun.

We **could** go swimming, **couldn't** we? – Yes, we **could**.

Form **Positive: could; Negative: couldn't/could not**

For short answers ▷ 7.2

Use We use **could** to talk about possible actions in the future.

▷ 34.2,4 (Communication: requests and suggestions)

7.9 CERTAINTY: *WILL, MUST, CAN'T*

Mr Malik caught the ten o'clock train to Manchester, so he'**ll** be there now/he **must** be there now.

You **must** be mistaken. I saw him half an hour ago, so he **can't** be in Manchester.

Form ▷ 4.1 *(will)*; 7.4 *(must)*; 7.2 *(can)*

Use We use **will/won't, must** and **can't** when we know something (e.g. *He caught the train)* which tells us that what we are saying is true.

He'll be/He must be there now. = He is certainly there now.
He can't be there. = He is certainly not there; it is impossible.

▷ 33.4 (Communication: being sure and unsure)

7.10 IMAGINING SITUATIONS: *WOULD*

A holiday in the Bahamas **would** be nice. –
Yes, it **would**. **I'd** lie in the sun all day. –
How much **would** it cost? –
Well, it **wouldn't** be cheap.

Form **Would** in all persons.

Short forms
'd = would **wouldn't** = would not

Short answers
Yes, I/you/he/we/they **would**.
No, I/you/he/we/they **wouldn't**.

Use We use **would** to talk about a situation which we are imagining (= thinking about) but which is not really happening.

▷ 7.12 (other uses); 16.2 (*would like*); 33.7 (Communication: imagining)

7.11 HABITS: *WILL, WOULD*

1 Mr Bell gets very tired in the evenings. He**'ll** often go to bed at nine o'clock.
2 When he was younger he **would** often stay up until after midnight.

Form **Will** (▷ 3.1) and **would** (▷ 7.10) in all persons.

Use
1 We sometimes use **will** to talk about a habit (something that happens **again and again**). But ▷ 2.4
2 We sometimes use **would** to talk about a habit in the past.

This meaning of **would** is almost the same as **used to**. ▷ 3.11
We use **would** for past habits mostly in written English.

7.12 USES OF *WOULD* AND *SHOULD*

Would		
Imagining situations	It **would** be nice to have a party here one weekend.	▷ 7.10
Past habits	Every afternoon the old man **would** go for a walk.	▷ 7.11
Improbable or **unreal actions**	If I had a lot of money, I'**d** travel round the world.	▷ 11.1
Reporting *will*	Sarah said she **would** come tomorrow.	▷ 12.3
Wishes	I wish this rain **would** stop.	▷ 13.3
Requests	**Would** you write your address here, please?	▷ 34.2
Invitations	**Would** you like to come to dinner? – Yes, I'**d** like to very much.	▷ 34.12
Preferences	I'**d rather** have tea than coffee.	▷ 35.4
Should		
Obligation	We **should** help other people.	▷ 7.6
Improbable future actions	If you **should** be late, I'll wait for you.	▷ 11.2
Advice	I think you **should** go by plane. It's much quicker.	▷ 34.5

▷ 4.10 (uses of *will* and *shall*)

7.13 *DARE*

1a **Dare** you climb this tree? – No, I **daren't**.
I **daren't** go so high.
b The boys **dared not** swim across the river.

2a **Do** you **dare (to)** climb this tree? – No, I **don't**.
I **don't dare (to)** go so high.
b The boys **didn't dare (to)** swim across the river.

Form

1 We can use **dare/dared** as a modal verb.
We use the infinitive without **to** after the modal verb.

2 We can use **dare** as a full verb with **do/did**.
We use the infinitive with or without **to** after the full verb.

Use

Dare means not to be afraid.

We use **dare** mostly in questions and negative sentences.

7.14 MODAL VERBS + *BE* + -ING FORM

Obligation:	Why are you sitting here watching television? You **ought to be doing**/**should be doing** some work.
Probability: **(present)**	Where's Jane? – I don't know. Perhaps she's doing some shopping. Or she **may be visiting**/**might be visiting** her friend Elaine.
(future)	Elaine **may be coming**/**might be coming** for tea tomorrow.
Certainty:	What's that noise? – It's Mr Greaves. He **must be repairing** his motorbike.
Imagining:	I'm glad it's a holiday. I**'d be learning** English at school if it wasn't.

We use a modal verb + the continuous form (**be** + -ing form) to talk about things that are (or are not) happening now or about future actions *(may/might be doing)*.

▷ 4.6 (future continuous: *will be doing*)

7.15 MODAL VERBS + *HAVE* + -ED FORM

Necessity:	Not many people came to the party – we **needn't have bought** so much food. (= It was not necessary to buy so much food, but we had bought it.)
Obligation:	Peter and Susan didn't come. They **ought to have told** us./**should have told** us. (= They had an obligation to tell us, but they didn't tell us.)
Probability:	They **may have forgotten**/**might have forgotten** about it. (= It is probable that they forgot about it.)
Possibility:	But Susan mentioned the party yesterday. She **couldn't have forgotten** about it. (= It isn't possible that she forgot about it.)
Imagining:	It **would have been** nice to see them here. (= . . . if we had seen them here.)

We use a modal verb + the perfect form (**have** + past participle) to talk about things in the past.

NOTE We **needn't have bought** so much food.
(= We bought too much.)
We **didn't need to** buy much food.
(= We didn't buy much because there was no need.) ▷ 7.4

▷ 4.9 (future perfect: *will have done*), 11.1 (if-clauses)

7.16 BE ABLE TO, BE ALLOWED TO AND HAVE (GOT) TO

1 **Simple and perfect tenses**

Present	I'**m able to** get about more easily because I've got a car now. I **don't have to** go on the bus.
Past	I **was allowed to** use my own car when I took the driving test.
Present perfect	I **haven't had to** take a teacher with me since I passed the test. I'**ve been allowed to** drive alone.
Past perfect	I **hadn't been able to** travel much before I bought the car.

2 **Continuous tenses**

Present continuous	I'**m having to** pay a lot for repairs these days.
Past continuous	But before I had a car, I **was having to** wait for the bus every evening.

3 **After** will, might **etc**

Future with will	I don't know the way, so I'**ll have to** look at the map.
Other modal verbs	I **might be allowed to** leave work early on Friday. I **may have to** start earlier in the morning. You **ought to be able to** get here by eight o'clock.

1 We can use **be able to** (▷ 7.2), **be allowed to** (▷ 7.3) and **have (got) to** (▷ 7.4) in simple and perfect tenses.

2 We can use **have to** in continuous tenses.

3 We can use **be able to, be allowed to** and **have (got) to** after **will** and other modal verbs.

8 Negatives, questions and tags

8.1 NEGATIVE STATEMENTS

1a I'**m not** feeling very warm, and I **haven't** brought a coat.
b We **can't** go back now or we **won't** get there in time.
c Oh, it **doesn't** matter. I **didn't** want to go back.

2a	There are **no** lights on.	There aren't any lights on.
b	Peter isn't here, and **neither** is Jane.	Peter isn't here, and Jane isn't either.
c	I can see **nobody** in the house.	I can't see anybody in the house.
d	I've **never** been here before.	I haven't ever been here before.

1 In a negative statement we use **n't/not** after

a the auxiliary verbs **be** or **have** ▷ 5.8
b a modal verb ▷ 7.1
c the auxiliary verb **do** in the simple present and simple past ▷ 2.4; 3.3; 5.8

▷ 1.2 (word order)

2 We can also make a negative statement with

a **no** (▷ 20.12) and **none** (▷ 20.18)
b **neither** and **nor** (▷ 9.1; 27.4)
c **no one, nobody, nothing** and **nowhere** (▷ 20.14)
d **never** (▷ 24.11)

8.2 QUESTIONS

Yes/no questions	W-questions
1 **Are** you looking for somewhere to eat? **Has** the new restaurant opened yet?	Where **are** you going? Which café **have** you been in before?
2 **Shall** we have lunch now? **Will** John have time?	How **can** we get there? When **must** John be back?
3 **Do** you normally come here? **Did** you see Tracy yesterday?	Why **does** Mr Gray eat so early? Who **did** you see in George Street? You saw somebody.
	4 Who **saw** you in George Street? Somebody saw you.

In questions we put one of these verbs before the subject:

1 the auxiliary verbs **be** or **have** ▷ 5.8
2 a modal verb ▷ 7.1
3 the auxiliary verb **do** in the simple present and simple past ▷ 2.4; 3.3; 5.8

(but see note 4)

1-3 **Yes/no questions** begin with an auxiliary or modal verb, and we can answer them with **yes** or **no**. ▷ 8.4
W-questions begin with a question word (▷ 21) and an auxiliary or modal verb.

4 But when **who** or **what** asks about the subject, the verb is the same as in a statement, e.g. *Who saw you . . . ?* ▷ 21.2

Alternative questions

5 **Are** you looking for somewhere to eat, **or** are you going home?

6 **Shall** we have lunch now **or** later?

7 **Did** your friends come here **or** go into town yesterday?

5-7 **Alternative questions** begin with an auxiliary or modal verb and have **or** (▷ 27.4) before the last alternative.

▷ 1.3 (word order); 39.3,4 (questions in statement form, intonation)

8.3 NEGATIVE QUESTIONS

1a Why **hasn't** Mr Robinson come?
b Who **isn't** here yet?

2a Why **don't** we ask Sarah to the party?
b Why **doesn't** she come on the bus?

3a You were reading that book last month. **Haven't** you finished it yet? – No, it's taking me a long time.
b **Don't** you like it? – Oh, yes, I like it very much.

4a **Didn't** you say you were going out with Tony? (= You said you were going out with Tony, didn't you?)
b **Isn't** that Tony coming now? (= That's Tony coming now, isn't it?)

Form In negative questions we use an auxiliary or modal verb + **n't**. ▷ 8.2

Use

1 We can use a question word in a negative question to ask for information.

2 We can use *Why don't/doesn't... ?* to make a suggestion. ▷ 34.4,9 (Communication)

3 A negative question can express surprise. *Haven't you finished it?* = I am surprised that you haven't finished it. ▷ 35.5 (Communication)

We use **no** to agree with a negative question, e.g. *Haven't you finished it?* – No, *I haven't finished it.*

We use **yes** to disagree with a negative question, e.g. *Don't you like it?* – Yes, *I like it very much.*

4 We can use a negative question to ask if a person agrees with a statement. ▷ 8.5

8.4 ANSWERING QUESTIONS

Yes/no questions

Have you seen the film?

1 Yes.	2 Yes, I have.	3 Yes, I have seen it.

Could you understand it?

1 No.	2 No, I couldn't.	3 No, I couldn't understand it.

W-questions

Who likes cowboy films?

1 Me.	2 I do.	3 I like cowboy films.

Where did you see the film?

1 At the Palace.		3 We saw it at the Palace.

We can answer questions

1 in one word or phrase.

2 often with a short answer using an auxiliary or modal verb.

3 with a full sentence.

Short answers are much more usual than full sentences.

▷ 34.2,4,11,12 (Communication: answering requests etc)

8.5 QUESTION TAGS

1a It's lovely today, **isn't it**? – It certainly is.
b You'll be on holiday next week, **won't you**? – No, we've had our holiday.
c Bob likes this weather, **doesn't he**? – Yes, he does.

2a We haven't had a nice summer for ages, **have we**? – No, we haven't.
b This weather can't go on much longer, **can it**? – I don't know.
c You didn't buy these drinks, **did you**? – No, Bob did.

Form We form question tags with

a the auxiliary verbs **be** or **have**,
b a modal verb, or
c the auxiliary verb **do** in the simple present or simple past.

In a negative tag we put **n't** after the auxiliary or modal verb.
After the verb (**+ n't**) there is a pronoun. The pronoun refers to the subject of the sentence.

Use 1 After a **positive statement** we use a **negative tag** to ask if a person agrees with the statement. ▷ 33.1 (Communication)

2 After a **negative statement** we use a **positive tag** to ask if a person agrees with the statement. ▷ 35.5 (Communication: showing surprise)

We use a falling intonation when we think the statement is true and we are asking someone to agree with it. (But he/she may disagree.)
We use a rising intonation when we are not so sure that the statement is true. A tag with a rising intonation is almost the same as a real yes/no question. ▷ 8.2

3a Ann isn't here. – Oh, she's working, **is she**?
b She won't be long. – She'll be back soon, **will she**?
c David's at work too. – So he works afternoons now, **does he**?

3 After a **positive statement** we can use a **positive tag** when we have just found out or just remembered some information and we want to ask or check if it is correct.
▷ 35.5 (Communication: showing interest)

We use a rising intonation in this kind of positive tag.

4a	Let's have some fresh air, **shall we**? I'll open the window, **shall I**?
b	Open the door too, **will you**?/**would you**?/**can you**?/**could you**?

4a After suggestions with **let's** and after offers, we use a tag with **shall**.

b After an imperative we use a tag with **will, would, can** or **could**.

These tags have a rising intonation.

9 Replacing words and leaving out words

9.1 SHORT ADDITIONS TO STATEMENTS

1 I like mountains. –
So do I./I **do, too**.

2 We've never been to Scotland before. –
Neither have we./**Nor have** we./We **haven't either**.

3 The boys had a holiday in spring. –
The girls **didn't**, though.

4 My brother can't swim, but *I* **can**.

5 My sister's going to Scotland. – Oh, **is** she?

1 We make positive additions to positive sentences with **so** or **too** and an auxiliary or modal verb.

2 We make negative additions to negative sentences with **neither/nor** or **either** and an auxiliary or modal verb.

We also use an auxiliary or modal verb for

3 negative additions to positive sentences

4 positive additions to negative sentences

5 short questions after statements ▷ 35.5 (Communication: showing surprise and interest)

9.2 *SO* AND *NOT* AFTER A VERB

1 Someone must have stolen your bicycle.	–	Yes, I suppose **so**.
2 Will the police get it back for you?	–	I don't think **so**.
3 Will you be able to buy a new one?	–	No, I'm afraid **not**.

1 We can use **so** after some verbs instead of a whole clause. *I suppose so.* = I suppose someone must have stolen my bicycle.

2 We can use **so** after the negative form of some verbs, e.g. **suppose, think, expect.**

3 We can use **not** to give a negative answer after some verbs, e.g. **be afraid, suppose, hope, believe, guess** (USA).

9.3 LEAVING OUT WORDS A

My sister plays the piano and my brother the guitar.
(= … and my brother **plays** the guitar.)

I like the music but not the words.
(= … but **I don't like** the words.)

Someone's borrowed that record and I don't know who.
(= … and I don't know who**'s borrowed it**.)

We can leave out words instead of saying them again if the meaning is clear without them.

▷ 8.4 (answering questions), 9.1,4; 14.13 (the verb after *to*); 18.4 (the possessive form); 20.18 (quantifiers without a noun)

9.4 LEAVING OUT WORDS B

Enjoying the music? – Sounds great.
(= **Are you** enjoying the music? – **It** sounds great.)

In informal speech we can leave out words from the beginning of a sentence if the meaning is clear without them.

The words which we leave out are usually a pronoun and/or an auxiliary verb.

10 The passive

10.1 THE PASSIVE: SIMPLE TENSES

The simple present tense

		Subject	Verb	Object	
Active:		The factories	pollute	the rivers	every day.
Passive:		The rivers	**are polluted**		every day.
Active:	Do	the companies	break	the law ?	
Passive:	**Is**	the law	**broken**?		

The simple past tense

		Subject	Verb	Object	
Active:		People	heard	the bomb	five miles away.
Passive:		The bomb	**was heard**		five miles away.
Active:	Did	the bomb	injure	many people ?	
Passive:	**Were**	many people	**injured**?		

Form We form the passive with **be** and the -ed form (past participle), e.g. *are polluted, is broken, was heard, were injured.*

The object of an active verb becomes the subject of a passive verb, e.g. *the rivers, the law.*

If the subject of a passive verb is plural, then the verb is also plural, e.g. *The rivers* are *polluted.*

The subject of the active verb (the **agent**) is left out of these passive sentences. ▷ 10.2

Use We use the passive to make the object of the active verb more important. It becomes more important when we put it at the beginning of the sentence.

10.2 THE BY-AGENT

		Subject	Verb	Object		(by-agent)
1	**Active:**	Bad driving	causes	accidents.		
	Passive:	Accidents	**are caused**		by	bad driving.
2	**Active:**	Motor cars	kill	children.		
	Passive:	Children	**are killed**		by	motor cars.
3	**Active:**	Someone	stole	the car.		
	Passive:	The car	**was stolen**.			
4	**Active:**	The police	arrested	the driver.		
	Passive:	The driver	**was arrested**.			

1,2 The subject of the active verb is the **agent**, the person or thing that does the action.

The agent can come after the passive voice in a phrase with **by** (the by-agent), e.g. *by bad driving, by motor cars.*
We put in the by-agent if it is important to mention the agent.

3 We can leave out the by-agent if we do not know the agent, e.g. *The car was stolen.* (We do not know who stole it.)

4 We can leave out the by-agent if we do not need to mention it, e.g. *The driver was arrested.* (We know that the police arrested him or her.)

10.3 THE PASSIVE: PERFECT TENSES

The present perfect tense

Active: They have opened two new motorways.
Passive: Two new motorways **have been opened**.

Active: How much has the government spent on them?
Passive: How much **has been spent** on them?

The past perfect tense

Active: They had planned the road ten years before work began.
Passive: The road **had been planned** ten years before work began.

Form We form the passive of perfect tenses with **have/has been** + past participle and **had been** + past participle.

Use ▷ 10.1

10.4 THE PASSIVE: CONTINUOUS TENSES

The present continuous tense

Active: They're painting the bridge at the moment.
Passive: The bridge **is being painted** at the moment.

The past continuous tense

Active: They were cleaning it when I crossed it last week.
Passive: It **was being cleaned** when I crossed it last week.

Form We form the passive voice of continuous tenses with **am/are/is being** + past participle and **was/were being** + past participle.

Use ▷ 10.1

10.5 THE PASSIVE: *WILL* AND OTHER MODAL VERBS

Breakfast **will be brought** to your room if you wish.
Meals **cannot be served** after 11.00 pm.
Your key **should be given** in before 11.30 am.
Must the bill **be paid** in cash?

Form After modal verbs we use **be** + past participle to form the passive.

Use ▷ 10.1

10.6 THE PASSIVE: DIRECT AND INDIRECT OBJECTS

Direct object
1a The company offered [a 10% wage increase] to the union.
b [A 10% wage increase] was offered to the union.

Indirect object
2a The company offered a 10% wage increase [to the union].
b [The union] was offered a 10% wage increase.

Direct object
1a They promised the workers [better conditions].
b [Better conditions] were promised to the workers.

Indirect object
2a They promised [the workers] better conditions.
b [The workers] were promised better conditions.

The object of an active verb becomes more important when we make it the subject of a passive sentence. ▷ 10.1

The subject of a passive sentence can be either

1 the **direct object** of an active sentence or

2 the **indirect object** of an active sentence.

▷ 1.4; 18.3 (objects in active sentences)

10.7 THE PASSIVE WITH *GET*

Lots of people **get injured** in the home.

Mrs Daley **got hurt** last week when she dropped a saucepan of boiling water.

Did she **get burnt**? – Yes, her arm was badly burnt.

In informal English we sometimes use **get** in the passive instead of **be**.

10.8 *HAVE/GET SOMETHING DONE*

1 **have something done**

I **had** the car **repaired** today. –
Did you **have** it **serviced** too? –
No, I didn't. I'm **having** it **serviced** tomorrow. –
You ought to **have** it **washed** too. –
I usually wash it myself.

2 **get something done**

I **got** the car **repaired** today. –
Did you **get** it **serviced** too? –
No, I didn't. I'm **getting** it **serviced** tomorrow. –
You ought to **get** it **washed** too. –
I usually wash it myself.

Form 1 **have** + object + past participle

2 **get** + object + past participle

Have and **get** are full verbs. They can have a continuous form *(I'm having/getting it serviced)*, and questions and negatives are with **do** *(Did you have/get it serviced?)*.

For e.g. *I had repaired the car* ▷ 3.6 (the past perfect tense)

Use *I had/I got the car repaired* = I asked someone to repair the car (and they repaired it).

Get is a little more informal than **have**.

10.9 *IT* + PASSIVE VERB + CLAUSE

1	**Active:**	People say that Mrs Harding does her job well.
	Passive:	**It is said** that Mrs Harding does her job well. ▷ 10.10
2	**Active:**	They decided to make her the manager.
	Passive:	**It was decided** to make her the manager.

We can use **it** and the passive voice

1 before a clause with **that**. We can use these verbs: **say, think, believe** etc (▷ 10.10) and **agree, decide, arrange**.

2 before an infinitive. We can use these verbs: **agree, decide, arrange**.

We use **it** if we do not want to mention the subject (e.g. *people, they*).

▷ 20.2 (uses of *it*)

10.10 THE PASSIVE: *SAY, THINK* ETC

Active:	People say that Mrs Harding does her job well.
Passive:	Mrs Harding **is said to do** her job well. ▷ 10.9
Active:	They thought Mr Sullivan was too old for the job.
Passive:	Mr Sullivan **was thought to be** too old for the job.
Active:	Everyone believes that Mr Dix has left the country.
Passive:	Mr Dix **is believed to have left** the country.

We can use these verbs in the passive before an infinitive:

say, think, believe, know, expect, suppose, report, consider.

We use the passive if we want to make the subject of the reported clause (e.g. *Mrs Harding*) more important.

10.11 THE PASSIVE: *SEE, HEAR* ETC

1	**Active:**	A detective **saw** the woman **put** some clothes into her bag.
	Passive:	The woman **was seen to put** some clothes into her bag.
2	**Active:**	A detective **saw** the woman **putting** some clothes into her bag.
	Passive:	The woman **was seen putting** some clothes into her bag.

1 After verbs of perception (**see, hear** etc) in the passive, the infinitive is with **to**.

2 After verbs of perception in the passive we can also use the -ing form.

▷ 14.10 (the infinitive after the passive); 16.3 (the infinitive and the -ing form)

11 If-clauses

11.1 THE MAIN TYPES OF IF-CLAUSE

Type 1: if + the simple present tense, + will, can or **may/might**

Probable actions in the future

If you **leave** before ten, you**'ll catch** the train.
If you **don't hurry**, you **might miss** it.
Yes, I**'ll miss** it **if** I **sit** here much longer.
I **can get** a bus **if** I **miss** the train.

Use We use Type 1 to talk about **future** actions that the speaker thinks are **probable**. *If you leave before ten* means that it is quite probable that you will leave before ten.

Type 2: if + the simple past tense, + would, could or **might**

a **Less probable actions in the future**

If we **saved** £500, we**'d have** enough for a car next year.
We **might save** enough **if** you **worked** overtime.

b **Unreal actions in the present**

If we **were** rich, I**'d buy** a Rolls Royce.
We **could** get a car now **if** you **didn't spend** so much on clothes.

Use

a We use Type 2 to talk about **future** actions that the speaker things are possible but **not very probable**. *If we saved £500* means that it is possible that we will save £500 but not very probable.

b We also use Type 2 to talk about **unreal** actions in the **present**. *If we were rich* means that we are not rich.

Type 3: if + the past perfect tense, + would have, could have or **might have**

Impossible actions in the past

If it **had rained** yesterday, there **wouldn't** have been many people at the sale.
If I **hadn't been** ill, I **could have gone** yesterday.
I **might have bought** some trousers **if** I**'d seen** some.
Peter **would have gone** to the sale **if** he**'d been** here.

Use We use Type 3 to talk about **past** actions that **did not happen**. *If it had rained* means that it did not rain.

Types 1-3

The if-clause can come before or after the main clause. We usually put a comma (in writing) and make a pause (in speech) when the if-clause comes first. ▷ 27.1

NOTE **'d** is the short form of **had** and of **would**.
If you**'d** asked me, I**'d** have told you. = If you **had** asked me, I **would** have told you.

▷ 13.2 (the unreal present and past); 34.6,7 (Communication: warnings and threats)

11.2 OTHER TYPES OF IF-CLAUSE

1 if + a present tense, + the imperative

If it**'s raining, take** a coat.
Don't wear those shoes **if** you **want** to go walking.

Use To give orders etc ▷ 6.1

2 if + the simple present tense, + the simple present tense

If a car **goes** fast, it **uses** more petrol.
If you **don't wash** a car, it **gets** very dirty.

Use To talk about things that are always true.

3 if + the present continuous/present perfect tense, + a modal verb

If you**'re planning** a holiday, **I'll tell** you about ours.
If you **haven't been** to Wales, you **ought to go** there.

Use Many uses, e.g. offering, giving advice.

4 if + a modal verb, + a modal verb

If you **can't find** a cup, there **might be** one in the cupboard.
Well, David **can't use** this kitchen **if** he **won't wash** up.

Use Many uses, e.g. suggestions, permission.

5 if + will/would, + a modal verb

If you**'ll give** me your address, I **can send** you the information.
If you **would** kindly **wait** a moment, please, Mr Barnes **won't be** long.

Use To make a request ▷ 34.2

6 if + should, + a modal verb/the imperative

I think it's going to be nice, but **if** it **should rain**, we **can have** the meal inside.
I'll probably arrive on time, but **if** I **should be** late, please **don't wait** for me.

Use To talk about future actions which the speaker thinks are not very probable.

1-6 For the three main types of if-clause ▷ 11.1. There are many other types of if-clauses with different verb tenses. These six types here are some of the most usual ones.

12 Reported speech

12.1 REPORTING VERBS

Statements

Direct speech:	1a	'There's a game this evening.'
Reported speech:	b	Peter **says** that there's a game this evening.
	c	There's a game this evening, Peter **says**.
Direct speech:	2a	'It begins at eight o'clock.'
Reported speech:	b	Jane **told** me it began at eight o'clock.
	c	It begins at eight o'clock, Jane **told** me.

Questions

Direct speech:	3a	'What time is the game?'
Reported speech:	b	David **asked** me what time the game was.

Statements

Say (1) and **tell** (2) are reporting verbs which report statements or thoughts. We also use **mention, answer, agree, write, think, know, be sure**.

Say does not have an indirect object. **Tell** must have an indirect object, e.g. *me*.

The reporting verb (e.g. *says*) usually comes before the reported clause (e.g. *there's a game this evening*), but the reported clause can come first (c). ▷ 27.1 (clauses)
When the reporting verb comes first, we can use **that** (1b) or leave it out (2b). Leaving it out is more informal.
When the reporting verb comes after the reported clause, we cannot use **that**.

Questions

Ask (3) is a reporting verb which reports questions. We also use: **wonder, enquire, want to know**.

▷ 12.6 (reporting orders and requests); 37.3 (comma); 37.5 (quotation marks)

12.2 REPORTING IN THE PRESENT TENSE

Tim is telling his parents what is in a letter from his friend John.

John's letter:	Tim:
I'**m having** a great time in New York.	John says he'**s having** a great time in New York.
My parents **like** it **here**, too.	He mentions that his parents **like** it **there**, too.
We'**ll be** home **next Tuesday**.	He says they'**ll be** home **tomorrow**.

When the reporting verb is in the present tense *(says, mentions)*, then the tense of the verb in direct speech *('m having, like, 'll be)* does not change.

Sometimes pronouns, adjectives and adverbs change in reported speech, e.g. *I → he, my → his, here → there, next Tuesday → tomorrow.*

We have to change these words when the situation has changed, e.g. New York is **here** for John but **there** for Tim because Tim is in England; the day when John comes home is **next Tuesday** for John but **tomorrow** for Tim because Tim reads the letter on Monday.

12.3 REPORTING IN THE PAST TENSE (A)

Elaine is reporting Tracy's words to Jim.

1 Tracy (to Elaine): We **need** Jim.
Elaine (to Jim): Tracy said they **needed** you.

2 Tracy (to Elaine): **I'm starting** a pop group.
Elaine (to Jim): She told me she **was starting** a pop group.

3 Tracy (to Elaine): I **haven't found** anyone who can play the guitar.
Elaine (to Jim): She said she **hadn't found** anyone who could play the guitar.

4 Tracy (to Elaine): **I'll be** at the club.
Elaine (to Jim): She told me she**'d be** at the club.

5 Tracy (to Elaine): The group **is going to meet** there.
Elaine (to Jim): She said that the group **was going to meet** there.

6 Tracy (to Elaine): I **must talk** to Jim.
Elaine (to Jim): She said she **had to talk** to you.

7 Tracy (to Elaine): He **played** in a group once.
Elaine (to Jim): She mentioned that you **had played**/that you **played** in a group once.

8 Tracy (to Elaine): It **would be** great if he **could play** in our group.
Elaine (to Jim): She said it **would be** great if you **could play** in their group.

If the reporting verb is in the past tense (e.g. *said, told*), then the verb in direct speech changes from the **present** to the **past** tense, e.g.

1 *need → needed*	4 *'ll → 'd*
2 *'m → was*	5 *is → was*
3 *haven't → hadn't*	6 *must → had to*

7 If the verb in direct speech is in the **past** tense, it either changes to the past perfect tense (e.g. *played → had played*) or it stays the same.

8 **Would, could, should, might** and **ought to** stay the same.

For **say** and **tell** ▷ 12.1.

12.4 REPORTING IN THE PAST TENSE (B)

Paul is reporting Sarah's words to Bob, the captain of the swimming team.

Sarah (to Paul): Swimming **is** my favourite sport.

Paul (to Bob):
1 Sarah said swimming **was** her favourite sport.
2 Sarah said swimming **is** her favourite sport.

Sarah (to Paul): I **can** swim two miles.

Paul (to Bob):
1 She told me she **could** swim two miles.
2 She told me she **can** swim two miles.

1 After a reporting verb in the past, there is usually a tense change. ▷ 12.3

2 But sometimes the verb in direct speech stays in the same tense if the words are still true when someone reports them, e.g. it is true that swimming **is** still Sarah's favourite sport.

Even if the words are still true, **we can always change the tense** into the past after a past tense reporting verb.

12.5 REPORTING QUESTIONS

One morning a man telephoned Jill's house. Jill's father wasn't in, so Jill answered the phone. When her father came home in the evening, she reported the conversation to him.

1 **Yes/no questions**

Voice on the phone: Is your father in?
Jill (to her father): A man on the phone asked **if** you were in.

Voice on the phone: Has he gone to London?
Jill (to her father): He wanted to know **whether** you'd gone to London.

2 **W-questions**

Voice on the phone: Which train did he take?
Jill (to her father): He asked me **which** train you'd taken.

Voice on the phone: When does he usually get home?
Jill (to her father): He asked **when** you usually got home.

1 We report yes/no questions with **if** or **whether**.

2 In w-questions we use question words (e.g. **which, when, what, who** and **how**) both in direct speech and in reported speech.

Verbs in reported questions change in the same way as in reported statements. ▷ 12.3

The word order in a reported question is the same as in a direct statement (not a direct question), e.g. *you were in, you'd gone to London, you'd taken, you usually got home.*

▷ 8.2 (questions); 21 (question words)

12.6 REPORTING ORDERS AND REQUESTS

1	Doctor (to Mr Smith):	Take your medicine after meals.
	Mr Smith (to his wife):	The doctor **told me to take** my medicine after meals.
2	Doctor (to Mr Smith):	You mustn't smoke.
	Mr Smith (to his wife):	He **told me not to smoke**.

1,2 We report orders (▷ 34.1) with **tell** + object + infinitive.

3	Doctor (to Mrs Smith):	Please don't buy your husband cigarettes.
	Mrs Smith (to her husband):	The doctor **asked me not to buy** you cigarettes.
4	Doctor (to Mrs Smith):	Could you get the medicine for him please?
	Mrs Smith (to her husband):	He **asked me to get** the medicine for you.

3,4 We report requests (▷ 34.2) with **ask** + object + infinitive.

5	Mr Smith:	I **was told to take** my medicine after meals.
	Mrs Smith:	I **was asked not to buy** you cigarettes.

5 The reporting verb can be in the passive. ▷ 14.10

6	Mr Smith:	The doctor said I **must** take/I **had to** take/I **was to** take my medicine after meals.
	Mr Smith:	He said I **mustn't** smoke./I **was not to** smoke.

6 We can also report orders with a form of **must** or **be to**.

7	Doctor (to Mrs Smith):	Can I have some water, please?
	Mrs Smith (to her husband):	He **asked me for**/He **asked for** some water.

7 We report a request **to have** something with **ask for**.

8	Mrs Smith:	He asked **if** I could get the medicine for you.
	Mrs Smith:	He asked **if** he could have some water.

8 We can also report requests which are in question form (e.g. *Could you...? Can you...?*) in the same way as other yes/no questions. ▷ 12.5

12.7 REPORTING SUGGESTIONS, ADVICE ETC

Suggestions	Let's go out. Tony **suggested going** out.	▷ 34.4
Advice	You'd better phone the police. Mrs Dell **advised me to phone** the police.	▷ 34.5
Warnings	Don't be late. I **warned you not to be** late.	▷ 34.6
Threats	If you don't go, I'll call the police. I **threatened to call** the police.	▷ 34.7
Insisting	We simply must take a taxi. Mr and Mrs Beal **insisted on taking** a taxi.	▷ 34.8
Promises	I'll send you a postcard. He **promised to send** us a postcard.	▷ 34.10
Offers	Can I get you a taxi? Eric **offered to get** the visitors a taxi.	▷ 34.11
Refusals	I'm not going to wait any longer. Mrs Janner **refused to wait** any longer.	▷ 34.11
Invitations	Would you like to have lunch with us? The Updikes **invited us to** lunch.	▷ 34.12

13 Tenses in main clauses and sub clauses

13.1 PRESENT AND PAST TENSES

1a We**'ll find** the place if we **buy** a map.
 b We**'d find** the place if we **bought** a map.

2a Kay **says** we**'ve taken** the wrong road.
 b Kay **said** we**'d taken** the wrong road.

3a Why **can't** we go the way I **want** to go?
 b Why **couldn't** we go the way I **wanted** to go?

If we change the tense in the main clause from present to past, we usually have to change the tense in sub clauses, e.g.

1 a sub clause with **if, when, because** etc
2 a reported clause
3 a relative clause

We use the simple present tense in sub clauses to talk about the future, e.g. *if we buy a map* (1a).

▷ 11 (if-clauses); 12 (reported speech); 27 (conjunctions)

13.2 THE UNREAL PRESENT AND PAST

1a Just suppose we **were staying** at the Hilton. (= but we aren't staying there.)
b You talk as if we **had** lots of money. (= but we haven't got lots of money.)
c It's time we **found** a room. (= but we haven't found one yet.)

2a If we**'d booked** one, we'd have been all right. (= but we didn't book one.)
b I'd rather we **hadn't come**. (= but we have come.)

After certain words or phrases (e.g. *suppose, as if*) we use

1 the past tense to talk about the unreal present.
2 the past perfect tense to talk about the unreal past.

▷ 11 (if-clauses); 13.3; 33.7 (Communication: imagining)

13.3 TENSES AFTER *WISH*

1 I wish you **wouldn't spend** so much money on cigarettes.
I wish you**'d smoke** a pipe instead.

2 I wish things **weren't** so expensive.
I wish we **could afford** a new car.

3 I wish I **hadn't lost** my job last month.
I wish I**'d saved** more money.

1 **Wish** + **would** is a wish for something in the **future**.
2 **Wish** + the past tense is a wish for something in the **present**.
3 **Wish** + the past perfect tense is a wish for something in the **past**.

▷ 35.3 (Communication: wishing)

14 The infinitive

14.1 THE INFINITIVE WITH *TO* AND WITHOUT *TO*

1a Are you ready **to go** now?
b Don't forget we've a bus **to catch**.
c I don't want **to be** late.
d They expect us **to arrive** at seven.
e Do you know where **to go**?

2a I must **finish** this homework.
b Our English teacher makes us **work** very hard.
c I'd better **do** it tonight.

The infinitive is the basic form of the verb, e.g. *go, catch, be.* We use it with **to** or without **to**.

1 The infinitive is with **to** after

a adjectives ▷ 14.2
b nouns ▷ 14.3
c verbs ▷ 14.4
d verb + object ▷ 14.5
e question words ▷ 14.12

2 The infinitive is without **to** after

a modal verbs ▷ 7.1
b **make** + object and **let** + object ▷ 14.8
c **had better** ▷ 34.5, and **would rather** ▷ 35.4

14.2 THE INFINITIVE AFTER ADJECTIVES

1 I'm glad **to see** you all.
2 It's too hot **to stay** in.
3 It would be better **to go** out.
4 The Top Club is easiest **to find**.

1,2 The infinitive after an adjective is with **to**.

3,4 We can also use the comparative and superlative of adjectives *(better, easiest)*.

14.3 THE INFINITIVE AFTER NOUNS AND PRONOUNS

Have you got a book **to read**?	(= a book you **can** read)
You'll need something **to eat**.	(= something you **can** eat)
I have some letters **to write**.	(= letters I **must** write)
There's lots of work **to do**.	(= work I **must** do)

The infinitive after a noun or pronoun is with **to**.

14.4 THE INFINITIVE AFTER VERBS

I've decided **to do** a course in nursing.
I hope **to get** a job near here.
I want **to find** somewhere to live.
I've arranged **to look** at a flat tomorrow.

For a list of verbs + infinitive with **to** and verbs + -ing form ▷ 16.1

14.5 THE INFINITIVE AFTER VERB + OBJECT

Andy's father wouldn't **allow** him **to use** the car.

He **persuaded** his parents **to buy** him a car of his own.

They **expected** him **to save** some money first.

He **invited** Eric and Alice **to go** for a ride.

Some other verbs which can have an object and an infinitive with **to** are: **tell, ask** (▷ 12.6), **want** (▷ 14.6), **warn, advise, teach, force**.

▷ 14.10 (passive)

14.6 *WANT SOMEONE TO DO SOMETHING*

Do you **want me to cook** the dinner?

I**'d like you to help** if you can.

Want and **would like** can have an object and an infinitive with **to**.

We cannot use a clause with **that** after **want** or **would like**.
We cannot change these sentences into the passive.

▷ 14.7; 34.1 (Communication: orders); 35.3 (Communication: wishing)

14.7 VERB + INFINITIVE WITH AND WITHOUT A NOUN PHRASE

We want to visit the Wilsons. (**We** visit the Wilsons.)	I expected to get a letter from them. (**I** get a letter.)
We want **the Wilsons** to visit us. (**The Wilsons** visit us.)	I expected **them** to write to us. (**They** write to us.)

We put a noun phrase (e.g. *the Wilsons, them*) before the infinitive when the subject of the sentece (We *want*, I *expected*) is not the same as the subject of the infinitive (the Wilsons *to visit us*, them *to write to us*).

▷ 14.11 (*for* + noun phrase + infinitive)

14.8 THE INFINITIVE WITHOUT *TO: MAKE* AND *LET*

The government **forced** companies **to hold** down wage increases.
The government **made** companies **hold** down wage increases.

They **allowed** workers **to have** only a 5% increase.
They **let** workers **have** only a 5% increase.

The verbs **force** and **allow** + object have the infinitive with **to**. ▷ 14.5

The verbs **make** (= force) and **let** (= allow) + object have the infinitive without **to**.

▷ 6.2 *(let's)*; 16.3 (after *see, hear* etc); 34.5 *(had better)*; 35.4 *(would rather)*

14.9 *HELP*

Can I **help** you **to pick** the apples?
Well, you could **help** Paul **dig** the garden.

The infinitive after **help** can be with **to** or without **to**.

14.10 THE INFINITIVE AFTER THE PASSIVE

1a The college **forced** the students **to work** hard.
b The students **were forced to work** hard.

2a The teachers **made** everyone **take** the exam.
b Everyone **was made to take** the exam.

3a They **let** the students **use** dictionaries in the exam.
b The students **were allowed to use** dictionaries in the exam.

After a passive verb the infinitive is always with **to** (b).

We do not use the verb **let** in the passive. Use the verb **allow** instead (3).

▷ 10.10 (*say, think* etc); 10.11 (*see, hear* etc)

14.11 *FOR* + NOUN PHRASE + INFINITIVE

1 It was easy **for the player to kick** the ball into the empty goal.
(= The player easily kicked the ball into the empty goal.)

2 It was a mistake **for Lewis to play** instead of Harper.
(= Lewis played instead of Harper, and that was a mistake.)

3 We are still waiting **for them to win** a game.
(= They have not won a game yet.)

We use **for** + noun phrase + infinitive after

1 an adjective, e.g. *easy*

2 a noun, e.g. *a mistake*

3 a verb which usually has **for** after it, e.g. *wait for.*

The noun phrase after **for** *(the player, Lewis, them)* is the subject of the infinitive.

14.12 THE INFINITIVE AFTER QUESTION WORDS

I don't know **how to get** to Glasgow. (= . . . how I **can** get to Glasgow.)

Can you tell me **where to buy** a ticket? (= . . . where I **can** buy a ticket?)

Do you know **what to say**? (= . . . what you **should** say?)

I've no idea **which bus to take**. (= . . . which bus I **must** take.)

I can't decide **whether to go** or not. (= . . . whether I **should** go or not.)

We can use the infinitive after question words and after **whether**.

14.13 LEAVING OUT THE VERB AFTER *TO*

Are you going to drive your father's car?
I'd like **to**, but I'm not allowed **to**.

We can leave out the verb after **to** if the meaning is clear without it. ▷ 9.3

14.14 OTHER FORMS OF THE INFINITIVE

Continuous infinitive

Those men seem **to be repairing** the road.
They oughtn't **to be making** so much noise on a Sunday.

Form **to be** + -ing form ▷ 7.14 (modal verbs + *be* + -ing form)

Perfect infinitive

I should like **to have walked** along the beach, but it's been raining.
We ought **to have spent** our holiday in a nice sunny place.

Form **to have** + -ed form (past participle)
▷ 7.15 (modal verbs + *have* + -ed form), 35.7 (Communication: regret)

Passive infinitive

I'm going **to be interviewed** next week.
I hope **to be offered** a job.

Form **to be** + -ed form (past participle) ▷ 10.5 (modal verbs)

15 The -ing form

15.1 THE -ING FORM AS A VERB-NOUN

1a **Smoking** isn't allowed here.
b I find **reading** difficult on a train.
c There's lots of time for **talking**.

2 **Driving** a car isn't as comfortable as **travelling** by train.

1 We can use the -ing form in the same way as other noun phrases. We can use it

a as a subject
b as an object
c after a preposition

2 After an -ing form we can put an object *(a car)* or an adverb phrase *(by train)*.

▷ 34.1 (Communication: written orders)

15.2 THE -ING FORM AFTER CONJUNCTIONS AND PREPOSITIONS

1 **After working** all evening, John felt tired.
On finishing his homework, Dick immediately went to bed.
We like a hot drink **before going** to bed.
Susan always has the radio on **while doing** her homework.
Judy hasn't found a job **since leaving** school.

2 **Although feeling** tired, David wanted to finish his work.
In spite of trying so hard, I always make mistakes.

3 Can't I watch television **instead of working**?
You won't pass the exam **without doing** any work.

4 I've got a special book **for writing** exercises in.

5 Jane stayed awake **by drinking** black coffee.

The clause with the -ing form can come either before or after the main clause.

1,2 Using the -ing form to express time or contrast is a little formal. In speech we often use a clause with a subject, eg. *after he'd worked all evening, although he felt tired.*

▷ 17.2; 27.2 (clauses of time); 27.6 (clauses of contrast)

3-5 We use the -ing form after **instead of, without, for** and **by** even in informal speech.

▷ 27.7 (clauses of reason); 27.8 (clauses of purpose); 25.9 (means)
▷ 17.5 (the -ed form after conjunctions; 34.4,12 *(What about/How about . . . ?)*

15.3 THE -ING FORM AFTER VERBS

Have you finished **writing** the letter?
Barry suggested **going** for a walk.
I don't mind **waiting** a few minutes.
We enjoy **walking**.

For a list of verbs + -ing form and verbs + infinitive ▷ 16.1

15.4 THE -ING FORM AFTER VERB/ADJECTIVE + PREPOSITION

1 **Verb + preposition + -ing form**

I'm **thinking of buying** an electric guitar.
My brother's **talking about starting** a new pop group.
He's **succeeded in finding** one or two people.

2 **Adjective + preposition + -ing form**

My sister's **fond of playing** music.
She's **good at writing** songs, and she sings at concerts.
She's **used to singing** in front of a lot of people.

1 More examples of verb + preposition which can have an -ing form (or a noun) after them:
worry about, believe in, insist on, feel like, agree with, look forward to, take part in.

2 More examples of adjective + preposition which can have an -ing form (or a noun) after them:
excited about, tired of, bored with, proud of, afraid of, interested in, keen on, pleased at.

15.5 THE -ING FORM WITH A SUBJECT

1a We've stopped **watching** television.
(= **We** don't watch television any more.)
b We've stopped **the children watching** television.
(= **The children** don't watch television any more.)

2a I insist on **having** a rest.
(= I insist that **I** have a rest.)
b I insist on **you having** a rest, Sarah.
(= I insist that **you** have a rest.)

3a I insist on **your having** a rest.
b I'm afraid of **Sarah's doing** too much.

1a, 2a When the subject of the sentence (*We've stopped*, I *insist*) is the same as the subject of the -ing form, we do not put the subject again before the -ing form.

1b, 2b When the subject of the sentence is **not** the same as the subject of the -ing form (The children *don't watch television,* You *have a rest*), we put a subject before the -ing form, too.

3 The subject of the -ing form can be a possessive form (e.g. *your, Sarah's*), especially if it is a pronoun or a name. A possessive form is more formal than e.g. *you, Sarah.*

15.6 THE PASSIVE -ING FORM

Visiting people is nicer than **being visited**.

I'm afraid of **being stopped** by the police if I drive too fast.

I don't like **being overtaken** by a Mini.

Form being + -ed form (past participle) ▷ 17.3 *(After being . . .)*

16 The infinitive and the -ing form

16.1 THE INFINITIVE AND THE -ING FORM AFTER VERBS

I wanted **to visit** England.
I enjoy **travelling** around.

After some verbs we use the infinitive with **to** (▷ 14.4), and after some verbs we use the -ing form (▷ 15.3).

Here are some of the most common verbs of both types.

+ the infinitive		+ the -ing form	
agree	learn	avoid	miss
arrange	manage	can't help	practise
can afford	offer	dislike	stop ▷ 16.2
choose	plan	enjoy	suggest
dare ▷ 7.13	promise	finish	
decide	refuse	go on	And: it's no fun
expect	seem	imagine	it's no good
fail	want	keep	it's no use
forget ▷ 16.2	wish	. . . n't mind/. . . mind . . . ?	it's worth
hope			

16.2 THE INFINITIVE AND THE -ING FORM: SPECIAL CASES

Mrs Scott **began to eat**/**began eating** her dinner.
She **intended to watch**/**intended watching** television after the meal.

After **begin, start, continue** and **intend,** we use either the infinitive or the -ing form. The meaning is the same.

I **like to have**/**like having** tea in front of the television.
I **love to read**/**love reading** at meal times.

After **like, love, prefer** and **hate,** we use either the infinitive or the -ing form. The meaning is the same. ▷ 35.2,3 (Communication: likes, dislikes and wishes)

I **like to go** to the doctor every year.
I **like to know** if there's anything wrong with me.

We use an infinitive after **like** to talk about something a person chooses to do but may not enjoy doing.

Dick **would like to stay** in, but I**'d prefer to sit** outside.

After **would like** (=want), **would love, would prefer** and **would hate,** we use the infinitive. ▷ 35.4 (Communication: preferences)

1a He **remembered to bring** the drinks.
b He **didn't forget to bring** the drinks.
2a I **remember having** a picnic here ten years ago.
b I'll **never forget having** a picnic here ten years ago.

1 We use an infinitive after **remember** or **not forget** when we first remember something and then do it (e.g. *bring the drinks).*
2 We use an -ing form after **remember** or **not forget** when we first do something and then remember it later.

remember (that you have to do something) + infinitive

remember (something you did in the past) + -ing form

1 I'm **trying to get** brown in the sun.
2 Why don't you **try putting** some cream on your back?

1 We use an infinitive after **try** when **try** means do your best to succeed *(to get brown).*
2 We use an -ing form after **try** when **try** means do something as a test *(putting some cream on your back)* to see if it will succeed (if it will make your back brown).

try (= make an attempt) + infinitive

try (= make the experiment of) + -ing form

1	I **stopped to get** this cream as I was driving from the hotel.
2	Your back'll **stop hurting** if you put some cream on.

1 We use an infinitive after **stop** when we want to say why someone stops. ▷ 27.8 (clauses of purpose)

2 We use an -ing form after **stop** to talk about an action no longer happening.

stop (in order to do something) + infinitive

stop (= finish doing something) + -ing form

▷ 35.6 (regret)

16.3 THE INFINITIVE AND THE -ING FORM AFTER *SEE, HEAR* ETC

1 We saw a group of people **climb** the mountain.
(= We saw them do the whole climb to the top.)
2 We saw a group of people **climbing** the mountain.
(But we did not see them do the whole climb.)
3 We heard a man. He shouted.
We heard a man **shout**.
(= He shouted once and we heard the shout.)
4 We heard a man. He was shouting.
We heard a man **shouting**.
(= He shouted a number of times and we heard some of the shouts.)

1,3 We use the infinitive without **to** after verbs of perception (**see, hear, watch, notice, listen to** etc) to talk about a complete action.

2,4 We use the -ing form after verbs of perception to talk about part of an action, but not the whole action from beginning to end.

▷ 10.11 (the passive)

17 The -ing form and the -ed form

17.1 THE -ING FORM AND THE -ED FORM USED AS ADJECTIVES

1a The gang ran out to the **waiting** car.
b The car almost ran into a **passing** lorry.

2a The **injured** man was taken to hospital.
b The **stolen** money was in **used** notes.

1 The -ing form (present participle) describes an action (The car **was waiting**).

2 The -ed form (past participle) describes the result of an action (The man **was injured**).

For e.g. *the car waiting outside* ▷ 22.11

▷ 29.7 (compound adjectives)

17.2 TIME: THE -ING FORM

1a Jane ate her supper while she was sitting in front of the television.
b She heard the telephone and got up to answer it.

2a Jane ate her supper **while sitting** in front of the television.
b **On hearing** the telephone, she got up to answer it.

3a **Sitting** in front of the television, Jane ate her supper.
b **Hearing** the telephone, she got up to answer it.

4 Jane ate her supper **sitting** in front of the television.

1 To talk about two actions that happen **at the same time** or that happen **one after the other**, we can use two clauses.

2 We can also use an -ing form after a conjunction or preposition. ▷ 15.2

3a We can use an -ing form without a conjunction or preposition to talk about an action that happens at the same time as another action.
b We can also use an -ing form without a conjunction or preposition to talk about an action that happens just before another action. The -ing form comes before the main clause.

4 If the actions happen at the same time, the -ing form can come after the main clause.

An -ing form before the main clause is rather formal, and we use it more in writing than in speech.

17.3 TIME: THE PERFECT -ING FORM

Remember:

1a After he had finished his work, the head teacher went home.
b After they had been shown round the school, the visitors had lunch.

2a **After finishing** his work, the head teacher went home.
b **After being shown** round the school, the visitors had lunch.

3a **Having finished** his work, the head teacher went home.
b **Having been shown** round the school, the visitors had lunch.

Form
3a The perfect -ing form (active): **having** + -ed form.
3b The perfect -ing form (passive): **having been** + -ed form.

Use
1 Remember that we use the past perfect tense to talk about the first of two actions in the past. ▷ 3.6; 10.3

2 We can use **after** + the active or passive -ing form in the same way. ▷ 15.2

3 We can also use the perfect -ing forms without **after** to talk about the first of two actions in the past.

The sentences with -ing forms are more formal than the sentences with a past perfect tense.

17.4 REASON: THE -ING FORM AND THE -ED FORM

1a I began to walk more quickly because I didn't want to be late.
b I began to walk more quickly, not **wanting** to be late.

2a As I was prevented from hurrying by the crowds, I decided to take a bus.
b **Prevented** from hurrying by the crowds, I decided to take a bus.

3a Because I had worked late, I hadn't got home until seven.
b **Having worked** late, I hadn't got home until seven.

4a As I had been asked to stay on at work, I had missed my train.
b **Having been asked** to stay on at work, I had missed my train.

We can use the -ing form and the -ed form to give a reason (b). ▷ 27.7

We can use these forms:

1b the -ing form
2b the -ed form (which has a passive meaning)
3b the perfect -ing form (active) ▷ 17.3
4b the perfect -ing form (passive) ▷ 17.3

The -ing form and the -ed form are more formal than the clauses with **because** and **as**.

17.5 THE -ED FORM AFTER CONJUNCTIONS

Although sold at a high price, the car was in poor condition.
(= Although it had been sold . . .)

Motorists may not stop on the motorway **unless forced** to do so.
(= . . . unless they are forced . . .)

The -ed form has a passive meaning.

We can use the -ed form after **although, unless, if, when** and **till/until**.

The clause with the -ed form can come either before or after the main clause.

Using the -ed form is more formal than using a subject and verb, e.g. *it had been sold, they are forced.*

▷ 15.2 (the -ing form after conjunctions and prepositions)

18 Nouns

18.1 REGULAR PLURALS OF NOUNS

my hat	our hat**s**	this box	these box**es**
a book	book**s**	a watch	some watch**es**
a dog	some dog**s**		
one day	two day**s**		

▷ 30.1 (pronunciation); 30.2,3,6 (spelling)

The regular plural ending is **-s/-es**.

18.2 IRREGULAR PLURALS OF NOUNS

1	a potato	some potato**es**
	a tomato	a pound of tomato**es**

We add **-es** after **o** in **potato, tomato, hero, Negro**. But **photo, piano** and **radio** are regular (**photos, pianos, radios**).

2	a knife	the kni**v**es	[vz]
	the shelf	the shel**v**es	[vz]

[f] becomes [vz] in **knife, shelf, wolf, thief, calf, half, wife, life, leaf, loaf**. But **chief, cliff** and **roof** are regular (**chiefs, cliffs, roofs**).

3	his mouth	their mouths	[ðz]
	a path	two paths	[ðz]

[θ] becomes [ðz] in **mouth, path, bath, youth.** But **birth, death** and **month** are regular [θs].

4	a house	a lot of houses	[zɪz]

House [s] becomes **houses** [zɪz].

5	her child	her child**ren**	[ˈtʃɪldrən]
	an ox	two ox**en**	

Child and **ox** have a plural in **-en**.

6	a sheep	some sheep
	an aircraft	two aircraft

Sheep, deer, most names of fish (e.g. **salmon, trout**) and **aircraft, spacecraft** and **hovercraft** have the same singular and plural form.

7	a foot	six feet	[fi:t]
	a tooth	teeth	[ti:θ]
	the goose	the geese	[gi:s]
	a mouse	some mice	[maɪs]
	the woman	the women	['wɪmɪn]
	a man	two men	[men]
	a policeman	three policemen	[mən] (+ postmen, milkmen etc)

In some words the vowel changes and there is no **-s**.

8	one penny	ten pence (an amount ▷ 31.9) ten pennies (= ten penny coins)
	a person	people persons (formal)
	a fish	a lot of fish (the normal plural form) three fishes (less usual; sometimes = three different kinds of fishes)

Penny, person and **fish** have two plural forms.

▷ 18.12 (pair nouns); 18.13 (nouns with a plural form); 23.10 (nationality words)

18.3 DIRECT AND INDIRECT OBJECTS

(What did Debbie give her mother/her father?)

1a Debbie gave **her mother the scarf** for Christmas.
 b She gave **her the scarf**.

2a She bought **her father the cigars**.
 b She bought **him the cigars**.

(Who did she give the scarf/the cigars to?)

3a She gave **the scarf to her mother**.
 b She gave **it to her mother**.
 c She gave **it to her**.

4a She bought **the cigars for her father**.
 b She bought **them for her father**.
 c She bought **them for him**.

1,2 The indirect object without **to** or **for** comes before the direct object.

3,4 The indirect object with **to** or **for** comes after the direct object.

3 We use **to** with **give, send, hand, pass, bring, take, pay, lend, write, show** and **tell**.

4 We use **for** with **buy, get, bring, find** and **make**.

We can use a pronoun
1b, 2b instead of an indirect object
3b, 4b instead of a direct object
3c, 4c instead of both an indirect object and a direct object

▷ 10.6 (passive)

18.4 THE POSSESSIVE FORM

1 **Singular**

This is my father's car. –
And whose is that? – It's Mrs Green's.

2 **Plural**

Is that a girls' school or a boys' school? –
It's for girls *and* boys. The Atkinsons' children go there.

3 **Plural without** -s/-es

The men's toilets are near the children's playground.

Form

1 With singular nouns we use an apostrophe **+ s**: **'s**.

2 With plural nouns we put an apostrophe after the **s**: **s'**.

3 With irregular plural nouns that do not end in **-s/-es** we use an apostrophe **+ s**: **'s**.

We can leave out the noun if the meaning is clear without it, e.g. *It's Mrs Green's* = It's Mrs Green's car.

Use

We use the possessive form with persons to show that something **belongs** to somebody (*My father's car* means that my father has a car.) or that something is **for** somebody (*a girls' school* = a school **for** girls). But ▷ 18.6

▷ 30.1 (pronunciation); 30.6 (with *-y*)

18.5 THE POSSESSIVE FORM IN PHRASES OF PLACE

Have you been to the chemist's?
No, I've been at the Wilsons' all afternoon.

the chemist's = the chemist's shop
the Wilsons' = the Wilsons' house/the Wilson family's house

18.6 THE POSSESSIVE FORM IN PHRASES OF TIME

I read about the strike in **yesterday's** paper.
The workers have lost a **week's** wages.
They want five **weeks'** holiday.
It's a 15 **minutes'** drive to the factory.

yesterday's paper = the paper that came out yesterday
a week's wages = wages for a week
five weeks' holiday = a holiday that lasts five weeks
a 15 minutes' drive = a distance that we can drive in 15 minutes

For *15-minute drive* ▷ 29.8

18.7 *OF* USED INSTEAD OF THE POSSESSIVE FORM

1 **With things**

There were people picnicking on **the bank of the river**.
It was **the beginning of the holidays**.

2 **With people**

We could hear **the voices of children** playing in the water.
The car park was full with **the cars of all the people** who had come out for the day.

1 We use **of** instead of the possessive form before the name of a **thing** (▷ 18.4). We use it to show that something (e.g. *the bank*) belongs to or is part of another thing (e.g. *the river*).

2 We use **of** instead of the possessive form with **people** when the noun has a phrase or clause after it which describes the noun, e.g. *children* playing in the water.

For *the river bank* ▷ 23.11

18.8 COUNTABLE AND UNCOUNTABLE NOUNS

1 **Countable nouns**

a We need **a teapot** and **some cups**. We don't need **spoons**.
b Here's **the teapot**, and here are **our cups**.
c There are **two cups**.

2 **Uncountable nouns**

a We need **some milk** and **some tea**. I don't take **sugar**.
b Here's **the milk**, and here's **our tea**.
c There are **two bottles of milk**.

1 **Teapot, cup** and **spoon** are countable nouns. Countable nouns have a plural form, e.g. *cups*. ▷ 18.1

We can say
a **a cup, some cups, cups**
b **the cup, the cups; my cup, your cup** etc
c **two cups, three cups** etc

2 **Milk, tea** and **sugar** are uncountable nouns. Uncountable nouns do **not** have a plural form. (But ▷ 18.10)

We can say
a **some milk, milk**
b **the milk; my milk, your milk** etc

2c We cannot use a number + uncountable noun. To say **how much** milk, we use a countable noun + **of**, e.g. *two bottles of milk*. ▷ 18.9

▷ 18.10; 19.2 (*a/an, the* and *some*); 20.12 (*some, any* and *no*); 20.15 (*a lot of, many, much*)

18.9 COUNTABLE AND UNCOUNTABLE NOUNS: *OF* IN PHRASES OF QUANTITY

1 **Countable nouns**	2 **Uncountable nouns**
a box **of** matches two packets **of** cigarettes	a bottle **of** milk two tins **of** meat
a kilo **of** apples six pounds **of** potatoes	half a pound **of** butter five gallons **of** petrol
	a drop **of** water two pieces **of** paper
	a bar **of** chocolate three loaves **of** bread

We use a noun (e.g. *box, packets*)) + **of**:

1 with a countable noun when it is easier to say how many e.g. *boxes* or *kilos.*

2 always with an uncountable noun (e.g. *milk, meat*) to talk about quantity (to say **how much** milk or meat).

▷ 20.15 (*a lot of*); 20.19 (quantifiers + *of*)

18.10 UNCOUNTABLE NOUNS MADE COUNTABLE

1a Two cups of tea and one cup of coffee, please.
b **Two teas** and **one coffee**, please.

2a We had different kinds of wine and cheese.
b We had different **wines** and **cheeses**.

1 We sometimes use uncountable nouns as countable nouns when we are ordering drinks or food.

2 We can also use uncountable nouns as countable nouns when we are talking about **a kind of** or **kinds of** wine, cheese, fruit, wool etc.

18.11 UNCOUNTABLE NOUNS: *INFORMATION, NEWS, ADVICE*

Someone's given me **some** interesting **information**/told me **some** exciting **news**/given me **some** good **advice**.

I've got an interesting **piece of information**/two or three **bits of news**/a **bit of advice** for you, too.

Information, news and **advice** are uncountable nouns. To say **how much** information etc, we use **piece** or **bit + of**.

Note also: a **piece of homework**, a **piece of furniture**, a **bit of progress**.

18.12 PAIR NOUNS

1 Look at **these tights** here.
I need **some trousers**.
My glasses are broken.

2 I need **a pair of trousers**.
I've already got about **five pairs of jeans**.

1 Pair nouns (e.g. *tights, trousers*) are always plural.

2 If we want to say **how many,** we use **pair/pairs + of**.

Other pair nouns: **scissors, pyjamas, shorts, pants**.

18.13 OTHER NOUNS WITH A PLURAL FORM

1 **Always with a plural verb**

His clothes were old and dirty.
The goods are still at the docks.

2 **Always with a singular verb**

Mathematics is a difficult subject.
The news is at ten o'clock on ITV.

3 **With a plural or a singular verb**

The company's **headquarters is/are** in Leeds.
The cheapest **means** of transport **is** the bicycle/**are** the bicycle and the motorcycle.

Other nouns that have a plural form but no singular form are

1 Always with a plural verb: **riches, thanks, contents**

2 Always with a singular verb: **measles, politics, athletics**

3 With a plural or a singular verb: **works** (= factory)

18.14 COLLECTIVE NOUNS

1a **The family has** lived here for hundreds of years.
b **The family have** all gone on holiday to different places.

2 **The police have** got Mrs Kenyon's address.

1a We use the singular form of the verb after a collective noun (e.g. *family*) if we are thinking of the group as a whole.
b We use a plural verb if we are thinking of the group as a number of individual people.

2 The verb is always plural after **police** and **cattle**.

Other collective nouns:

group, gang, club, team, crowd, class, government, army, company.

18.15 NOUN PHRASES OF MEASUREMENT

350 miles was too far to drive in one day. **8 hours seems** a very long time in a car. – But it's cheaper than the train; **£65 is** very expensive.

We use the singular form of the verb after a noun phrase of measurement or amount.

19 The articles: *a/an* and *the*

19.1 THE PRONUNCIATION OF THE ARTICLES

a/an		**the**	
a school	[ə] + [s]	**the** school	[ðə] + [s]
a teacher	[ə] + [t]	**the** teacher	[ðə] + [t]
a new address	[ə] + [n]	**the** new address	[ðə] + [n]
a university	[ə] + [j]	**the** university	[ðə] + [j]
an apple	[ən] + [æ]	**the** apple	[ðɪ] + [æ]
an empty tin	[ən] + [e]	**the** empty tin	[ðɪ] + [e]
an hour	[ən] + [aʊ]	**the** hour	[ðɪ] + [aʊ]

We use **a** [ə] before a consonant sound and **an** [ən] before a vowel sound.

We use **the** [ðə] before a consonant sound and **the** [ðɪ] before a vowel sound.

19.2 *A/AN* AND *THE*

1 There's **a** man and some girls in the water.

2a **The man** is swimming, but **the girls** aren't.
b **The sun** is shining.
c **The beach** is empty now. **The water** is nice and warm.

1 We use **a/an** only with singular countable nouns. In the plural we use **some**. ▷ 19.3

A/an = one. *A man* = one man (but we don't know **which** man), a man not mentioned before.

2 We use **the** with countable nouns (singular and plural) and with uncountable nouns.

We use **the**:

a before nouns already mentioned. *The man* = the man I have just spoken about.

b before e.g. *sun* because there is **only one** sun.

c when it is clear that the speaker is talking about one special thing. *The beach* = this beach I am talking about (we know **which** beach).

19.3 *A/AN* AND *SOME*

Singular nouns

1a Look, there's **a horse** in the field.
b It's **a pony**, not a horse.
c **A horse** is bigger than a pony.

Plural nouns

2a I'm going to buy **some apples**.
b No, let's get **oranges** today.
c Well, **apples** are cheaper at the moment.

Uncountable nouns

3a Would you like **some tea**?
b Is this **tea** or coffee?
c I like **tea** best.

1a We use **a/an** only with singular countable nouns. **A/an** means **one**. ▷ 19.2

b We use **a/an** when we are talking about **what something is**, e.g. *a pony, not a horse.*

c We also use e.g. **a horse** to talk about **all horses**.

2a With plural nouns we use **some**. *Some apples* = a number of apples.

b We use a plural noun without **some** when we are talking about e.g. *oranges* (and not apples), and we are not interested in **how many** oranges.

c We also use a plural noun without **some** to talk about e.g. **all apples**.

3a We can also use **some** with uncountable nouns.

b We use an uncountable noun without **some** when we are talking about e.g. *tea* (and not coffee); and we are not interested in **how much** tea.

c We also use an uncountable noun without **some** to talk about e.g. **all tea**.

▷ 18.8 (countable and uncountable nouns); 20.3 (*it, one, them* and *some*)

19.4 PLACE NAMES WITH AND WITHOUT *THE*

1 **Continents** Have you been to **Africa**?		
2 **Countries** **England** is a small country. I come from **Canada**.	But:	**the** West Indies from **the** United States to **the** Netherlands in **the** USSR
3 **Lakes and mountains** Chicago is on **Lake Michigan**. Who first climbed **Mount Everest**?	But:	in **the** Highlands **the** Alps
4 **Rivers, canals and seas**		on **the** River Thames through **the** Suez Canal in **the** Atlantic Ocean
5 **Cities, towns and villages** We stayed in **New York**.	But:	in **the** Hague
6 **Streets, parks and bridges** in **Oxford Street** near **Piccadilly Circus** through **Hyde Park** **Tower Bridge**	But:	in **the** High Street **the** Oxford Road (= the road to Oxford) **the** Strand, **the** Mall
7 **Theatres, cinemas, hotels, museums and galleries**		**the** Shakespeare (Theatre) at **the** Classic (Cinema) **the** Hilton (Hotel) near **the** British Museum in **the** National Gallery
	And:	**the** Empire State Building
8 **Other buildings** to **Buckingham Palace** outside **Westminster Abbey** at **Shell-Mex House** near **Victoria Station** from **Heathrow Airport**	But:	at **the** White House
9 **Phrases with** *of* But: at London University		in **the** House of Commons at **the** University of London **the** England of Shakespeare

We do **not** use **the** before the names of

1 continents
2 countries
3 lakes and mountains
5 cities, towns and villages
6 streets, parks and bridges
8 buildings other than hotels, museums etc

We use **the** before

2,3 plural names and e.g. USSR, UK
4 the names of rivers, canals and seas
7 the names of theatres, cinemas, hotels, museums and galleries
9 phrases with **of**

19.5 UNCOUNTABLE NOUNS WITH AND WITHOUT *THE*

1 **Meat** is expensive.
2 **The meat at our supermarket** costs a lot.

1 **Crime** is increasing.
2 **The crime we read about** in the newspapers is terrible.

1 We can learn a lot from **history**.
2 This book is about **the history of Europe**.

1 We do not use **the** before an uncountable noun with a general meaning. *Meat* = all meat.

2 But we use **the** before an uncountable noun with a limited meaning, e.g. *the meat at our supermarket.*

▷ 18.8 (uncountable nouns)

19.6 PHRASES OF TIME WITHOUT *THE*

Years	
in **1978**; after **1984**	But: in **the** year 1978
Seasons	
Winter begins next week.	
It's nice here in **summer**.	Or: It's nice here in **the** summer.
Months	
since **May**; **January** is often cold.	But: **The** January of 1979 was very cold.
Special times of the year	
Easter is in April this year.	
Are you going away at **Christmas**?	
Days	
on **Tuesday**; before **Friday**	But: on **the** Tuesday before last
Parts of the day and night	
at **midday**; at **night**	But: in **the** morning; during **the** afternoon; in **the** evening; in **the** night
Meals	
We had eggs for **breakfast**.	But: I didn't like **the** breakfast we had this morning.
Dinner is at half past seven.	

▷ 25.3 (prepositions of time); 25.8 *(by)*

19.7 *SCHOOL, PRISON* ETC WITH AND WITHOUT *THE*

1 **School** is over at four o'clock.
2 **The school** cost a lot of money to build.

1 The man was sent to **prison** for stealing cars.
2 The visitors came out of **the prison**.

1 Mrs Maxwell is in **hospital**. She's very ill.
2 She's in **the new hospital**.

We sometimes leave out **the** before

school, prison, hospital, church, college, university, class, court, market, town, home, sea and **bed**.

1 We leave out **the** when we are talking about school, prison etc as an **institution**, and we are interested in what we use it **for**.

2 But we use **the** if we are talking about a school, prison etc as a **building**.

We must use **the** if there is a word or phrase describing the noun, e.g. *the new hospital.*

19.8 *A/AN* BEFORE JOBS, NATIONALITIES AND BELIEFS

1 Mr Malone is **a** writer and Mrs Stein is **an** artist.

2a He's **an** Englishman and she's **an** American.
b He's English and she's American.

3 He's **a** Catholic and she's **a** Protestant.

1 We use **a/an** before a noun saying what a person's job is.
We cannot leave out **a/an**.

2a We use **a/an** before a noun of nationality.
b We can also use an adjective to give a person's nationality. ▷ 23.10

3 We use **a/an** before nouns which say what a person believes in. ▷ 29.5

19.9 *A/AN* IN EXCLAMATIONS

What a beautiful day!
What a lovely view you've got from your house!

19.10 QUITE, SUCH, RATHER AND HALF

1 We had **quite a** good time at the party.
(= The party was quite good.)

2 Dick told **such a** funny story.
(= The story was so funny.)

3a It was **rather a** nice party.
b It was **a rather** nice party.

4a Dick and Sarah only stayed **half an** hour.
b We knew **half the** people there.

Quite and **rather** are adverbs of degree. For meanings ▷ 24.12.

19.11 *A/AN* IN PHRASES OF PRICE, SPEED ETC

These apples are forty pence **a** kilo.
You can only go at thirty miles **an** hour on this road.
I go shopping for clothes about five times **a** year.

In these phrases **a/an** means **each** or **every**.

20 Pronouns and quantifiers

20.1 PERSONAL PRONOUNS

	Subject forms	Object forms
1	**I**'ve got three bags.	Help **me** with the bags, please.
2	**You** need some money.	I'll give **you** 50p.
3	What about Philip? Where is **he**?	We're waiting for **him**.
4	And Jane? Is **she** coming?	This is **her** now.
5	What about the taxi? Where is **it**?	I can't see **it**.
6	**We**'re coming.	Don't forget **us**.
7	Where are the others? Are **they** coming?	Tell **them** to come now.

Form

	Singular		Plural	
	Subject	**Object**	**Subject**	**Object**
1st person:	**I**	**me**	**we**	**us**
2nd person:	**you**	**you**	**you**	**you**
3rd person:	**he**	**him**	**they**	**them**
	she	**her**		
	it	**it**		

Use

We use pronouns to talk about the speaker *(I, we)* or the person who we are speaking to *(you)*.
We also use a pronoun instead of a noun phrase when there is no need to say the full phrase *(he, she, it, they)*.

We use the object form when the pronoun is

1 the direct object
2 the indirect object ▷ 18.3
3 after a preposition
4 after **be**

1 **I/me** means the speaker.
2 **You** means the person or the people who we are speaking to.
3 We use **he/him** to talk about a boy or man or a male animal (if we know the animal's male name).
4 We use **she/her** to talk about a girl or a woman or a female animal (if we know the animal's female name).
5 We use **it** to talk about a thing or an animal. But ▷ 20.2
6 **We** means the speaker and another person or people.
7 We use **they/them** to talk about people or things.

20.2 USES OF *IT*

1a Where's my watch? Have you seen **it**?
b There's someone at the door. – **It**'s Bob.

2 **It**'s getting late and **it**'s still raining.

3 **It** seems that the Graysons aren't coming.

4a **It** would be silly to go out now.
(= To go out now would be silly.)
b But **it**'s strange that they haven't telephoned.
(= That they haven't telephoned is strange.)

5 **It** was Pamela who wanted to come.
(= *Pamela* wanted to come)

We use **it**

1a to talk about a **thing** (e.g. *my watch*).
 b to talk about a **person** when we want to find out who the person is. *It* = the person at the door.
2 as subject in sentences about time or the weather.
3 as subject before **seem, appear** and **happen**.
4 instead of a subject clause (e.g. *to go out now, that they haven't telephoned*) when the clause comes later in the sentence.
5 to give emphasis to a word or phrase, e.g. *Pamela.* ▷ 28.3

▷ 5.3 (*it/there* + be); 10.9 (*it* + passive verb + clause)

20.3 *IT, ONE, THEM* AND *SOME*

1a I've got the camera. I've got **it** here.
 b I must buy a film. I must buy **one** today.
2a I like these stamps. I like **them** better than the old ones.
 b I want some stamps. I want **some** for these letters.
3a The coffee's nice. Where did you get **it**?
 b We need some coffee. I'll get **some** today.

1a **the, this, my** etc + singular noun → **it**
 b **a/an** + singular noun → **one**
2a **the, these, my** etc + plural noun → **they/them**
 b **some** + plural noun → **some**
3a **the, this, my** etc + uncountable noun → **it**
 b **some** + uncountable noun → **some**

▷ 19.3 (*a/an* and *some*); 20.12 (*some, any* and *no*); 20.18 (quantifiers without a noun)

20.4 A SPECIAL USE OF *YOU, ONE* AND *THEY*

1 **You** can't buy food cheaply nowadays.
2 **One** always tries to find the cheapest places.
3a **They**'re building a new supermarket in town.
 b **They** ought to do something about the price of food.
 c **They** say the new supermarket's going to be cheap.
4 **People** say the new supermarket's going to be cheap.
5 A new supermarket is being built in town.

1 We sometimes use **you** to talk about people in general (= everyone), including the speaker.
2 We also use **one** to talk about people in general, including the speaker. **One** is more formal than **you**.
3a We sometimes use **they** to talk about a group of people if we do not need to say or if we do not want to say who they are.
 b We sometimes use **they** to talk about the government or people in authority.
 c We also use **they** to talk about other people in general.
4 We also use **people** to talk about other people in general.
5 We can use a passive sentence instead of an active sentence with **they**. ▷ 10.1,3,4,10

20.5 POSSESSIVE ADJECTIVES AND PRONOUNS

Possessive Adjectives	Possessive pronouns
That isn't **my** key.	**Mine**'s here.
Put **your** hands in **your** pockets.	My hands are warm, but **yours** are cold.
Here's Jim's coat. Give him **his** coat.	It isn't **his**. It's Bill's.
Mary wants **her** hat.	This is **hers**.
The house lost **its** roof in the storm.	
Can we have **our** records?	We want **ours**, too.
Where's the Arnolds' car? They want to sell **their** car.	**Theirs** is the blue Mini. The green car is the Grays'.

Form

my key	**mine**	**our** records	**ours**
your hands	**yours**		
his coat	**his**	**their** car	**theirs**
her hat	**hers**		
its roof			

We use possessive adjectives with a noun and possessive pronouns without a noun.

Use We use possessive adjectives and pronouns to show that something belongs to somebody (my *keys* means that **I have** a key).
We must use possessive adjectives and pronouns with parts of the body (e.g. *your hands*) and clothes (e.g. *your pockets*) if we know who the hands, pockets etc belong to.

▷ 21.1 (*Whose . . . ?*)

20.6 *OF* + POSSESSIVE PRONOUN

Laura is a friend **of mine**.	(= one of my friends)
I've got some records **of hers**.	(= some of her records ▷ 20.19)

20.7 REFLEXIVE PRONOUNS

It's nice here. **I**'m enjoying **myself**.

Can **you** feel **yourself** getting brown in the sun?

If Tony has any more ice-cream, **he**'ll make **himself** sick.

Tracy will be OK – **she** can look after **herself**.

I think **that bird**'s hurt **itself**.

We've found **ourselves** a nice place here.

Can **you** children help **yourselves** to sandwiches?

The children are behaving **themselves** today.

Form

myself	**ourselves**
yourself	**yourselves**
himself	**themselves**
herself	
itself	

The singular pronouns end in **-self**, e.g. *yourself*.
The plural pronouns end in **-selves**, e.g. *yourselves*.

Use We use a reflexive pronoun to talk about the same person or thing that we mentioned in the subject of the sentence.

NOTE **enjoy yourself** = have a good time
help yourself to sandwiches = take some sandwiches
behave yourself = not be silly or naughty

20.8 EMPHATIC PRONOUNS

The Queen herself visited the town last year.
I didn't see her **myself**.

Form The emphatic pronouns have the same form as the reflexive pronouns. ▷ 20.7

Use We use an emphatic pronoun to lay emphasis on a noun phrase, e.g. *the Queen, I.* ▷ 28.5

20.9 *THEMSELVES* AND *EACH OTHER*

Bob and Sarah can look after **themselves**.
(= Bob can look after himself, and Sarah can look after herself.)
Mrs Brooks and Mrs Johnson babysit for **each other**.
(= Mrs Brooks babysits for Mrs Johnson, and Mrs Johnson babysits for Mrs Brooks.)
Tracy and Alice play **each other's** records.
(= Tracy plays Alice's records, and Alice plays Tracy's records.)

20.10 DEMONSTRATIVE ADJECTIVES AND PRONOUNS

Demonstrative adjectives	**Demonstrative pronouns**
What about **this** tie here?	No, I don't like **that**.
I like **that** dress there.	Or **this**, here?
These shirts are nice, look.	**Those** are, too.
Those coats are expensive.	**These** here are cheaper.

Form

this tie here **these** shirts here	**this** **these**	**that** dress there **those** coats there	**that** **those**

This and **that** are singular; **these** and **those** are plural.
We can also use **one** and **ones** instead of a noun with demonstrative adjectives. ▷ 20.11

Use

We use **this** and **these** to talk about things near the speaker.
We use **that** and **those** to talk about things that are further away from the speaker.

20.11 *ONE* AND *ONES*

1 After an adjective
Do you want a long coat or a **short one**? – The **long ones** are nice, aren't they?

2 After **the**
This dress isn't as nice as **the one** you first looked at.
I don't like these dresses as much as **the ones** in the window.

3 After **every**
We've seen plenty of coats. You've looked at **every one** in the shop.

4 After **each**
They all look the same to me. **Each one** looks the same.

5 After a demonstrative adjective
Look at those shirts. Do you like **this one** or **that one**? –
These ones are nicer than **those ones**.

6 After **which**
You've seen all the hats. **Which one** do you want?
You've seen all the shoes. **Which ones** do you want?

We use **one** instead of a singular noun (a short coat → *a short one*).
We use **ones** instead of a plural noun (the long coats → *the long ones*).

We **must** use **one/ones** or a noun (we cannot leave it out):

1 after an adjective in a noun phrase
2 after **the**
3 after **every** ▷ 20.13

We can use **one/ones** (but we can leave it out):

4 after **each** ▷ 20.13
5 after a demonstrative adjective ▷ 20.10
6 after **which** ▷ 21.3

20.12 *SOME, ANY* AND *NO*

1a I've got **some** money.
b There are **some** oranges at the shop.

2a I haven't got **any** food. Have you got **any** water?
b There aren't **any** apples at the shop. Are there **any** bananas?

3a Would you like **some** water? – Yes, please.
b Can I have **some** bananas, please?

4a I have **no** food.
b There are **no** apples at the shop.

1 We use **some** in positive sentences.

2 We use **any** in negative sentences and in questions. But ▷ 20.13

3 We use **some** in questions when we think the answer will be *yes*, e.g. in offers (▷ 34.11) and requests (▷ 34.2).

4 **No** is more emphatic than **n't . . . any**.

We use these quantifiers with both uncountable nouns (a) and plural countable nouns (b). ▷ 18.8

▷ 20.18 (without a noun)

20.13 QUANTIFIERS: *EVERY, EACH* AND *ANY*

1 There is a prize-giving **every** year.
Every pupil has to be there.

2 One pupil from **each** class gets a prize.
Each prize-winner can choose a book.

3 You can choose **any** book you like.
Anyone can enter the competition.

1 We use **every** to talk about what the speaker sees as a large indefinite number of people or things. *Every pupil* = all the pupils.

2 We use **each** to talk about the individual people or things in a group. The group has a definite (and often small) number. ▷ 20.20

3 We use **any** to talk about one person or thing (but it doesn't matter which one) from a large indefinite number. *Any book* = it doesn't matter **which** book; any book you like.

When **any** has this meaning, it is stressed.
Compounds with **any-** can also have the same meaning (*anyone* = it doesn't matter who).
Any is also the negative of **some**. ▷ 20.12

20.14 COMPOUNDS WITH *EVERY-*, *SOME-*, *ANY-* AND *NO-*

1a **Everyone**'s/**Everybody**'s here.
b **Someone**'s/**Somebody**'s missing.
c Has **anyone**/**anybody** seen Dick?
d No, **no one**'s/**nobody**'s seen him.

2a Have you got **everything**?
b There's **something** in the corner, isn't there?
c No, I haven't forgotten **anything**.
d I've left **nothing** behind.

3a I've looked **everywhere** for the key.
b It must be **somewhere**.
c I haven't seen it **anywhere**.
d It's **nowhere** here.

1 We use **-one/-body** to talk about **people**.

2 We use **-thing** to talk about **things**.

3 We use **-where** to talk about **place**.

We use **any-** in negative sentences and questions. ▷ 20.12 But ▷ 20.13

4a Dick isn't here, but **everyone else** is. (= all the other people)
b There's **something else** that I've forgotten. (= another thing)

5a Is there **anything interesting** on television?
b There's **nowhere nice** to go for a walk here.

4 We can use **else** after these compounds.

5 We can use an adjective after these compounds.

NOTE In informal speech Americans sometimes use **everyplace, someplace, anyplace** and **noplace** instead of **everywhere** etc.

20.15 QUANTIFIERS: *A LOT OF, MANY, MUCH, A FEW, A LITTLE*

	Countable nouns		Uncountable nouns
	(a large number)	**a lot of**	(a large amount)
1	I've got **a lot of** records.		There's **a lot of** wine here.

1 We use **a lot of** in positive sentences with both countable and uncountable nouns.

	many (a large number)	**much** (a large amount)
2	How **many** books have you got? Have you got **many** books?/ a lot of books?	How **much** beer is there? Is there **much** beer?/a lot of beer?
3	I haven't got **many** books./a lot of books.	There isn't **much** beer./a lot of beer.
4	I've got **too many** records.	That's **too much** beer for me.

2 We usually use **many** and **much** in questions, (but we sometimes use **a lot of** if we think the answer will be *yes*.)
We use **many** with countable nouns and **much** with uncountable nouns.

3 We usually use **many** and **much** in negative sentences, (but we sometimes use **a lot of** in informal English.)

4 We use **many** and **much** after **too, very, so** and **as**.

	a few (a small number)	**a little** (a small amount)
5	I've only got **a few** books.	There's only **a little** beer.

5 We use **a few** with countable nouns and **a little** with uncountable nouns.

20.16 QUANTIFIERS: *MORE, MOST; FEWER, FEWEST; LESS, LEAST*

Countable nouns		Uncountable nouns
(a bigger number)	**more**	(a bigger amount)
Our team has won **more** games than your team.		Your club has got **more** money than our club.
(the biggest number)	**most**	(the biggest amount)
We've won the **most** games. (= more games than anyone else)		You've got the **most** money. (= more money than anyone else)

We use **more** and **most** with both countable and uncountable nouns.

Countable nouns	Uncountable nouns
fewer/less (a smaller number)	**less** (a smaller amount)
You've won **fewer** games/**less** games than we have. (= You haven't won as many games as we have.)	We've got **less** money than you have. (= We haven't got as much money as you have.)
fewest/least (the smallest number)	**least** (the smallest amount)
You've won the **fewest** games/ the **least** games. (= fewer/less games than anyone else)	We've got the **least** money. (= less money than anyone else)

We use **fewer/fewest** (or **less/least** in informal English) with countable nouns and **less/least** with uncountable nouns.

▷ 20.20 (*most*); 23.2 (*more* and *most* with adjectives)

20.17 QUANTIFIERS: *SOME MORE, ANOTHER*

Countable nouns	Uncountable nouns
some more	**some more**
Would you like **some more** sandwiches?	Would you like **some more** tea?
another	
Would you like **another** sandwich?	

We use **some more** with both countable and uncountable nouns.

We use **another** (= one more) with countable nouns.

20.18 QUANTIFIERS WITHOUT A NOUN

With countable nouns

I need some apples. Can you lend me **some**? We haven't got **any** in the house. I need **a lot**, but there are **none** at the shop. –
Well, I've got **a few**. How **many** do you want?

With uncountable nouns

I need some sugar. Can you lend me **some**? We haven't got **any** in the house. I need **a lot**, but there's **none** at the shop. –
Well, I've got **a little**/**a bit**. How **much** do you want?

We can leave out a noun after a quantifier when the meaning is clear without it.

We cannot use **no** without a noun. We use **none** instead.

▷ 20.11 (*every/each + one*); 20.12 (*some, any* and *no*); 20.15 (*a lot of, many, much, a few, a little*)

20.19 QUANTIFIERS + *OF*

With plural nouns

Most of the people in my class like sport, but not **all of them**.
A lot of the boys play football. **Some of them** play tennis. –
Do **any of them** play hockey? –
None of the boys do. –
How **many of the girls** play hockey? –
A few of them, I think, but less than **half of them**. **Two of the girls** play table-tennis, and **one of the boys** likes boxing.

With singular or uncountable nouns

I read **most of this book** last night, but not **all of it**. **A lot of it**'s very interesting, but I missed out **some of it**. –
Was **any of it** too hard to understand? –
No, **none of it** was very difficult. –
How **much of the book** have you read now? –
I've only got **a little of it**/**a bit of it** still to read. I've read more than **half of it**.

We use **of** when we talk about a quantity (e.g. *most*) which is part of another quantity (*the people in my class*).
We cannot use **no** + **of**. We use **none** + **of** instead.

▷ 20.15,20; 27.4 (*either, neither*)

20.20 *ALL, MOST, BOTH* AND *EACH*

1a **All parties** are exciting, I think.
b **All the guests**/**All of the guests** have arrived.
c The guests have **all** arrived.
d I've said hello to them **all**.
e They haven't drunk **all the wine**/**all of the wine** yet.
f They've drunk **all this bottle**/**all of this bottle**.
g They've drunk **this whole bottle**/**the whole of this bottle**.
h **All my friends**/**All of my friends** are here.

2a **Most people** like parties.
b **Most of the men** are drinking beer now.
c We've drunk **most of the wine** already.

3a **Both rooms**/**Both the rooms**/**Both of the rooms** are full.
b The rooms are **both** full.
c We're using the two rooms. We're using them **both**.
d **Both these bottles** are empty.
e **Both our children** are in bed.

4a **Each guest**/**Each of the guests** had a drink.
b The guests **each** had a drink.
c I gave them **each** a drink.
d These bottles cost £2 **each**.

1a **All** = every ▷ 20.13

All + noun (without **the**) has a general meaning. *All parties* = every party **in the world**.

b **All the** + noun and **all of the** + noun have a more limited meaning. *All the guests/ All of the guests* = all the guests **at this party**.

c,d We can use **all** in mid position or after an object pronoun.

e We can use **all** with uncountable as well as countable nouns.

f We can use **all** with **this, that, these** and **those**.

g We can use **whole** with a singular noun with the same meaning as **all**.

h We can use **all** and **all of** with **my, your** etc.

2a **Most** = more than half.

Most + noun (without **the**) has a general meaning. *Most people* = most people **in the world**.

b **Most of the** + noun has a more limited meaning. *Most of the men* = most of the men **at this party**.

c We can use **most** with uncountable as well as countable nouns.

▷ 24.5 (*most/mostly*)

3a We use **both** to talk about **two** things or **two** people. ▷ 27.4 (*either, neither*)

We can say **both** + noun, **both the** + noun or **both of the** + noun.

b,c We can use **both** in mid position or after an object pronoun.

d We can use **both** with **these** and **those**.

e We can use **both** with **my, your** etc.

4a We use **each** to talk about the individual things or people in a group. ▷ 20.13

We can say **each** + noun or **each of the** + noun.

b,c We can use **each** in mid position or after an object pronoun.

d We can use **each** in end position.

21 Question words

21.1 *WHAT, WHO, WHERE, WHEN, WHY, HOW* AND *WHOSE*

1 **What** are you doing here? – I'm looking for someone.
2 **Who** sent you here? – The manager.
3 **Where** is the manager now? – In London.
4 **When** did he go there? – Yesterday afternoon.
5 **Why** have you come? – Because I want to see Mr Black.
6 **How** did you get here? – I came by car.
7 **Whose** car is it?/**Whose** is it? – It's mine.

1 **What** asks about **actions** or **things**. ▷ 21.2,3
2 **Who** asks about **people**. ▷ 21.2,3
3 **Where** asks about **place**.
4 **When** asks about **time**.
5 **Why** asks about **reason** or **purpose**. ▷ 27.7,8
6 **How** asks about **means**. ▷ 25.9 Also ▷ 32.2,3 (Communication: introductions, saying hello).
7 **Whose** asks about **possession**.

21.2 *WHO* AND *WHAT* ASKING ABOUT THE SUBJECT AND THE OBJECT

Asking about the subject

1a Who wants cheese? – We all do.
(= **We all** want cheese.)
b What made that noise? – The washing-machine.
(= **The washing-machine** made that noise.)

Asking about the object

2a Who do you want here on Saturday. – Everybody.
(= I want **everybody** here on Saturday.)
b What did Sandy make? – A box.
(= Sandy made **a box**.)

1 When **who** or **what** asks about the subject, the verb is the same as in a statement, e.g. *wants, made.*
2 When **who** or **what** asks about the object, we use a form of **do** in the simple present or simple past tense.

NOTE We can use **who** or **what** with other tenses to ask about the subject, e.g. *Who's taken my pen? What's making that noise?*

21.3 *WHO, WHAT* AND *WHICH*

1 **Who**'s your favourite film star? – Paul Newman.

2a **What**'s your favourite sport? – Tennis.
b **What sport** do you like best? – I like tennis.
c **What hobbies** have you got? – I take photos, and I collect old coins.

3a **Which** is your favourite hobby, taking photos or collecting coins?
b **Which book** are your photos in? – This album here.
c **Which photos**/**Which ones** did you take in Germany? – The ones on this page.
d **Which of these girls**/**Which one** is your sister? – The one on the left.

Form 1 **Who** is always without a noun.

2 **What** can be
a without a noun
b with a singular noun
c with a plural noun

3 **Which** can be
a without a noun
b with a singular noun
c,d with a plural noun, with **one/ones** (▷ 20.11) or with **of** (▷ 20.19).

Use 1 **Who** asks about **people**.
2 **What** asks about **things**.
3 **Which** asks about things **or** people.

We use **who, what** or **which** when there is a number of possible answers to choose from. The difference between them is that:

1,2 We use **who** or **what** when there is an indefinite (and often very large) number of possible answers, or when we do not know the possible answers.
3 We use **which** when there is a limited (and often very small) number of possible answers to choose from.

21.4 QUESTION PHRASES WITH *WHAT* AND *HOW*

What kind of car is Mr Simon's? – It's a Ford.
What colour is it? – Blue.
What about his wife's car? – She drives a red Mini.
What time does she get home? – About half past five.

How old are you, Mr Hall? – Twenty-three.
How much do you earn? – A hundred pounds a week.
How many children have you got? – One.
How often do you have a holiday? – Once a year, usually.

These question phrases ask about the details of a person, a thing, or an action.

▷ 20.15 (*how much/how many*)

21.5 PREPOSITIONS IN QUESTIONS

1 **Which** office is Mrs Brooks working **in** now? – The small office.
(Mrs Brooks is working **in** the small office now.)

2 **Who** are you two talking **about**? – The new manager.
(We're talking **about** the new manager.)

3 **What** did she want you **for**? – Nothing important.

4 **What**'s she **like**? – She's very nice.

1,2 In a question we put a preposition in the same place as in a statement. We do not put it before the question word.

3 **What for**? = Why?

4 **What . . . like**? asks a question that we can answer with an adjective.

22 Relative clauses

22.1 RELATIVE PRONOUNS AND RELATIVE CLAUSES

1a The boy *who* **comes from Bristol** won the game.
b The sport *that* **I like watching** is tennis.

2a Peter Oates, *who* **comes from Bristol**, won the game.
b The first game, *which* **went on for a long time**, wasn't very exciting.

A relative clause (e.g. *who comes from Bristol*) begins with a relative pronoun (e.g. *who, that*). But ▷ 22.4,10,11
A relative clause comes after a noun (e.g. *the boy, the sport*) and tells us about the noun.

1 Most relative clauses are **defining clauses**, e.g. *who comes from Bristol* (without commas). ▷ 22.12
The relative clauses in 22.2-11 are defining clauses.

2 Some relative clauses are **non-defining clauses**, e.g., *who comes from Bristol,* (with commas). ▷ 22.12

22.2 THE RELATIVE PRONOUNS *WHO* AND *WHICH*

1 The girl *who* **works at the café** is John's sister.
Is that the café *which* **stays open till ten**?

2 John is the boy *who* **you met yesterday**.
Did you see the motor-bike *which* **he bought for £20**?

Who and **which** are relative pronouns. ▷ 22.1. We use **who** with people and **which** with things.

Who and **which** can be
1 the subject of a relative clause (**The girl** works at the café. **The café** stays open till ten.)
2 the object of a relative clause (You met **the boy** yesterday. He bought **an old motor-bike** for £20.)

22.3 THE RELATIVE PRONOUN *THAT*

1 Is this the train *that* **stops at Shenfield**?
Here's the newspaper *that* **I found on the seat**.

2 The man *that* **sat next to us yesterday** is a detective.
I think he was following the woman *that* **you helped**.

We can use the relative pronoun **that** instead of **who** or **which**. ▷ 22.2
1 We mostly use **that** to talk about things.
2 We sometimes use **that** to talk about people, but we use **who** much more often. ▷ 22.2

22.4 RELATIVE CLAUSES WITHOUT A PRONOUN: LEAVING OUT *WHO, WHICH* OR *THAT*

1a John is the boy *who* **you met yesterday**.
b John is the boy **you met yesterday**.
2a Did you see the motor-bike *which* **he bought for £20**?
b Did you see the motor-bike **he bought for £20**?
3a His sister works in the café *that* **we went to**.
b His sister works in the café **we went to**.

We can leave out **who, which** or **that**:
1,2 when it is the **object** of a relative clause (You met **the boy** yesterday. He bought **an old motor-bike** for £20.)
3 when there is a **preposition** (We went **to the café**.) ▷ 22.5

We cannot leave out **who, which** or **that** when it is the subject of the relative clause.
▷ 22.10,11 (relative clauses without a pronoun)

22.5 PREPOSITIONS IN RELATIVE CLAUSES

1 A girl **who** I used to go out **with** lives near here.
(I used to go out **with** a girl.)
2 The hotel **which** we stayed **at** yesterday wasn't very nice.
(We stayed **at** the hotel.)
3 Here's the map **that** you were looking **for**.
(You were looking **for** the map.)
4 The road you were talking **about** earlier is here on the map.
(You were talking **about** the road.)

In a relative clause we put a preposition in the same place as in a main clause. We do not usually put it before the relative pronoun. But ▷ 22.7

We can use a preposition in a relative clause
1 with **who**
2 with **which**
3 with **that**
4 without a pronoun

▷ 21.5 (prepositions in questions)

22.6 THE RELATIVE PRONOUN *WHOM*

The woman *who* **they interviewed yesterday** has been given the job.
The woman *whom* **they interviewed yesterday** has been given the job.

We use **who** and **whom** to talk about **people**.
We can use **whom** instead of **who** when it is the **object** of the relative clause (They interviewed **the woman** yesterday.)
Whom is more formal than **who** and is not often used in spoken English.
We can also use **whom** with a preposition. ▷ 22.7

22.7 A PREPOSITION AT THE BEGINNING OF A RELATIVE CLAUSE

1a The person *who* **I spoke** *to* **earlier** isn't there now.
b The person *to whom* **I spoke earlier** isn't there now.
2a It's a problem *which* **we can do very little** *about*.
b It's a problem *about which* **we can do very little**.

1a,2a In a relative clause we usually put a preposition in the same place as in a main clause. This is the normal order in informal spoken English. ▷ 22.5

1b,2b In more formal or written English we can put a preposition at the beginning of a relative clause.
If we put a preposition at the beginning, we use **whom** or **which**. We cannot use the relative pronouns **who** or **that** after a preposition.

22.8 THE RELATIVE PRONOUN *WHOSE*

1 Workers **whose** wages are low should be paid more.
2 We are a nation **whose** wealth comes mainly from industry.
3 The cow **whose** milk you've been drinking is in that field over there.
4a That's the farm **whose** owner went to Australia.
b That's the farm the owner **of which** went to Australia.

We use **whose** to talk about **possession**. *Whose wages* = the workers' wages.

We use **whose** to talk about

1 people
2 countries
3 animals
4 things

We also use **of which** to talk about things (4b).

22.9 THE RELATIVE PRONOUN *WHAT*

The manager never tells us **what** we need to know.
(= . . . the things that we need to know)
He never lets me do **what** I want to do.
(= . . . the things that I want to do.)

▷ 28.4 (*what* used for emphasis)

22.10 RELATIVE CLAUSES WITHOUT A PRONOUN: THE INFINITIVE

1 Gary was **the first** person **to arrive** and **the last to leave**.
(= . . . the first person who arrived and the last one who left.)
2 Jill was **the only** one **to wish** me a happy birthday.
(= . . . the only one who wished me . . .)
3 Your party was **the most exciting** thing **to happen** here for months.
(= . . . the most exciting thing that's happened here . . .)

We can use the infinitive instead of a relative pronoun and a verb

1 after **the first, the second** etc.
2 after **the only**
3 after superlatives

22.11 RELATIVE CLAUSES WITHOUT A PRONOUN: THE -ING FORM AND THE -ED FORM

1 People **wanting** to buy a house should ask at the office.
(= People who want to buy a house . . .)

2 The men **building** the houses were well paid.
(= The men who were building the houses . . .)

3 New homes **offered** for sale today are sold very quickly.
(= New homes which are offered for sale . . .)

4 A house **bought** ten years ago is worth much more today.
(= A house which was bought ten years ago . . .)

1,2 We can use an -ing form instead of a relative pronoun and an active verb.
3,4 We can use an -ed form instead of a relative pronoun and a passive verb.

The -ing form or the -ed form can replace a verb
1,3 in a present tense or
2,4 in a past tense

22.12 DEFINING AND NON-DEFINING RELATIVE CLAUSES

Defining relative clauses

1a The man **who has worked here for 45 years** is retiring next month.
b The company **he works for** is Wilson and Sons.

1 Most relative clauses are **defining clauses**. The clause *who has worked here for 45 years* defines the man (tells us **which** man).

The defining clause is necessary to understand the meaning of the sentence. There is no pause or comma before a defining relative clause.

Non-defining relative clauses

2a Mr Rose**, who has worked here for 45 years,** is retiring next month.
b Wilson and Sons**, for whom he has worked since he was 20,** have been in existence since 1823.
c The manager **(whose wife was also there)** handed a beautiful old clock to Mr Rose.
d The clock **– which cost over £100 –** was paid for by the people at the factory.

2 Some relative clauses are **non-defining clauses**. The clause, *who has worked here for 45 years,* adds extra information about Mr Rose. It does not define Mr Rose – we already know who he is. We can leave out the non-defining clause and still have a sentence which means something. There is a short pause (in speech) or a comma (in writing) before and after a non-defining relative clause. The clause is sometimes in brackets (2c) or between dashes (2d).
We form non-defining relative clauses with **who, whom, whose** or **which**. We do not use **that** in non-defining clauses.
Non-defining relative clauses are rather formal.

3 Mr Rose has worked here for 45 years, and he's retiring next month.

3 In informal spoken English we normally use two main clauses instead of a main clause and a non-defining relative clause.

22.13 *WHY, WHEN* AND *WHERE*

1a I've forgotten the reason **why** we went to Bournemouth.
. . . the reason we went to Bournemouth.
b I'll never forget the day **when** we arrived there.
. . . the day we arrived there.
c Do you remember the hotel **where** we stayed?
. . . the hotel we stayed at?
2a We went in May, **when** it's normally quiet.
b We stopped at Ashford, **where** there's that nice pub by the canal.

1 We can use **why, when** and **where** in a defining relative clause.
We can leave out **why** or **when** from a defining clause. We can also leave out **where**, but then we must use a preposition, e.g. *the hotel we stayed* at (1c).

2 We can form non-defining relative clauses with **when** and **where**.
We cannot leave out **when** and **where** from a non-defining clause.

22.14 *WHICH* REFERRING TO A WHOLE CLAUSE

I went out last night, **which** meant that I had no time for my homework.
I was late again this morning, **which** made my teacher angry.

We can use **which** to talk about a whole clause, e.g. *I went out last night, I was late again this morning.* These relative clauses with **which** are non-defining clauses.

23 Adjectives

23.1 THE FORM AND USE OF ADJECTIVES

1 That's a **nice** book. – Yes, I've got some **nice** books.
2 Is it a **good** story? – Yes, I think it's very **good**.

Form
1 An adjective has the same form in the singular and in the plural, e.g. *a nice book/ nice books.*
2 An adjective comes before a noun (*a good story*) or after **be** (*it's good*). And ▷ 24.6

Use An adjective describes (tells us something about) a noun.

23.2 THE REGULAR COMPARISON OF ADJECTIVES

1a This old record's **cheap**. It's only 30p.
b This one's **cheaper** than that. It's 25p.
c I've got **the cheapest** record in the shop. It's only 10p.
2a This is an **expensive** coat. It's £50.
b The blue one is a **more expensive** coat than the red one.
c This one is **the most expensive** of all. It's £100.
3a I've got a cheaper one **than Bob./than Bob has.**
b You've got a more expensive one **than him./than he has.**

1 Short adjectives (e.g. **cheap, fast, tall**) have **-er** in the comparative (*cheaper*) and **-est** in the superlative (*cheapest*).
2 Longer adjectives (e.g. **expensive, interesting, dangerous**) have **more** in the comparative (*more expensive*) and **most** in the superlative (*the most expensive*). ▷ 23.5 (*less* and *least*)
3a After the comparative form + **than** we can put a noun phrase + verb (*than Bob has*) or just a noun phrase (*than Bob*).
b A personal pronoun after **than** has the object form (*than him*).

NOTE

silly (+ happ**y**, funn**y**, dirt**y**, earl**y**)	**sillier**	the **silliest**
clever	**cleverer**	the **cleverest**
simple	**simpler**	the **simplest**
quiet	**quieter**	the **quietest**
careful (+ use**ful**, hope**ful**)	**more careful**	the **most careful**
modern	**more modern**	the **most modern**
correct	**more correct**	the **most correct**
boring	**more boring**	the **most boring**
famous	**more famous**	the **most famous**

With some adjectives we can use either **-er/-est** or **more/most**, e.g. **polite, stupid, narrow, complete, pleasant, common.** ▷ 30.3,5,6 (spelling)

23.3 THE IRREGULAR COMPARISON OF ADJECTIVES

1 Nottingham has some **good** shops, but Sheffield is **better**.
The shops in Manchester are the **best**.
2 Thursday is market day. It's a **bad** day for parking.
Friday is **worse**, and Saturday is the **worst** time.
3 It's a long way to Sheffield, but it isn't **far** to Nottingham. Manchester is **further/farther** from here than Sheffield, but Leeds is **the furthest/the farthest**.

Form

1 **good**	**better**	**best**
2 **bad**	**worse**	**worst**
3 **far**	**further/farther**	**furthest/farthest**

3 We use **far** in negative sentences and questions. We use **a long way** in positive sentences. ▷ 23.8 (*further/farther*); 24.8 (irregular comparison of adverbs)

23.4 COMPARISON: *AS . . . AS*

1 The weather is just **as** cold **as** last winter.
2a Today isn't **as** windy **as** yesterday.
b Today's not **so** windy **as** yesterday.

Form
1 In positive sentences we use **as . . . as**.
2 In negative sentences we use either **as . . . as** or **so . . . as**.

Use We use **as . . . as** to compare two things that are the same.

23.5 COMPARISON: *LESS, LEAST*

These shoes are expensive. They're £25.
The black ones are **less** expensive. They're £20.
These here are **the least** expensive. They're £10.

Less and **least** are the opposites of **more** and **most**. ▷ 23.2

23.6 COMPARATIVES WITH *AND*

This town's getting **bigger and bigger**.
The roads are becoming **more and more crowded**.
There are **more and more people** here every year.
I enjoy living here **less and less**.

We can repeat a comparative after **and** to talk about a change happening over a period of time.

23.7 COMPARATIVES WITH *THE*

The longer the hours that people work, **the more** they produce.
The higher our wages, **the better** our standard of living.
The more careful we are with our money, **the less likely** we are to get into difficulties.

We use **the** + comparative to talk about a change in one thing which causes a change in another thing.

23.8 *LATEST, LAST; NEAREST, NEXT; FURTHER, FARTHER; ELDER, ELDEST*

1a The M7 is our **latest** motorway. It was opened only last week.
b The M7 will be the **last** motorway. There's no money to build any more.

2a There are no garages here. The **nearest** one is 25 miles away.
b You'd better get some petrol at this garage. The **next** one is 25 miles away.

3a How much **further**/**farther** is it to Glasgow?
b Let's hope there are no **further** problems.

4a Have you an **older**/**elder** brother? – No, I'm the **oldest**/**eldest**.
b This car is **older** than your Mini was. It's the **oldest** one you've ever had.

1a **latest** = newest
b **last** = final (but *last week* = the week before this)

2a **nearest** = closest, least far
b **next** = the one after this

3a **further/farther** = longer
b **further** = more

4a We can use **elder/eldest** to talk about members of a family.
b We use **older/oldest** to talk about other people and things.

23.9 *THE* + ADJECTIVE

1 **The rich** are healthier than **the poor**.
(= rich people) (= poor people)

2 You've got to take **the good** with **the bad**.
(= good things) (= bad things)

3 **The good thing** about your idea is that it'll save money. But **the unfortunate thing** is that we have no time.

1 We use **the** + adjective to talk about a whole group of people e.g. **the young, the old, the sick, the unemployed**.

2 We also use **the** + adjective to talk about e.g. good things or bad things in general.

3 If we are talking about one special thing, e.g. an idea which is good, then we use **thing** after the adjective.

23.10 NATIONALITY WORDS

1a I've bought some **Italian** shoes.
 b Can you speak **Italian**?
 c A lot of **Italians** live in this part of town.

2a It's a **Japanese** radio.
 b I'm trying to learn **Japanese**.
 c A lot of **Japanese** come here in summer.

We can use a nationality word
a as an adjective
b as the name of a language
c to talk about people

1c Some of the words meaning people are nouns with a singular and a plural form, e.g. **an Italian, the Germans, some Swedes, an Englishman, two Englishmen, a Spaniard**.

2c Some of the words meaning people are adjectives which we also use as nouns, e.g. **the Japanese, a Chinese, all the Swiss, the English** (= English people), **the Spanish**. These adjectives do not have a plural form.

▷ 19.8 (*a/an*)

23.11 NOUNS USED AS ADJECTIVES

the **river bank**	= the bank of the river
the **kitchen door**	= the door of the kitchen
a **stone wall**	= a wall made of stone
a **London theatre**	= a theatre in London
a **school bus**	= a bus that goes to a school

River, kitchen etc are nouns used as adjectives.

Other examples: **garden gate, table leg, paper bag, gold watch, evening meal**.

▷ 18.7 (*the bank of the river*); 29.2 (compound nouns)

24 Adverbs

24.1 TYPES OF ADVERBS

1 **Adverbs of manner** ▷ 24.3
The children walked home **quickly**.
They ate their supper **hungrily**.

2 **Adverbs of time and place** ▷ 24.10
Mr Barnes is coming **tomorrow**.
He's going to have lunch **here**.

3 **Adverbs of frequency** ▷ 24.11
The Smiths **often** visit us.
They **usually** come on Sundays.

4 **Adverbs of degree** ▷ 24.12
I'm **very** tired.
I had to get up **really** early.
I **almost** fell asleep this afternoon.

5 **Adverbs referring to a whole sentence** ▷ 24.13
Maybe I'll go to bed.
I'll **probably** have a nice long sleep.
I don't need to get up early tomorrow, **luckily**.

We use an adverb
1 to say **how** something happens.
2 to say **when** or **where** something happens.
3 to say **how often** something happens.
4 to make the meaning of an adjective, adverb or verb **stronger** or **weaker**.
5 to refer to a whole sentence and show what the speaker thinks about the sentence.

▷ 24.9 (the position of adverbs); 26.1 (adverbs in phrasal verbs)

24.2 ADVERB FORMS

1a It'll be eight o'clock **soon**.
b Eric is **always** late.
c He wasn't **so** late last week.
d **Perhaps** he isn't coming.
2a We'll have to walk **fast**.
b We had to get up **early** this morning.
3a We'll have to walk **quickly**.
b I **usually** go this way.
c We're **nearly** at the house now.
d It's a bit further, **actually**.
4a The woman was friendly. She spoke **in a friendly way**.
b Rain is likely. It's **probably** going to rain.

1 Some adverbs have no special form. These adverbs are

a most adverbs of time and place ▷ 24.10
b some adverbs of frequency ▷ 24.11
c some adverbs of degree ▷ 24.12
d some adverbs referring to a whole sentence ▷ 24.13

2 Some adverbs have the same form as adjectives. These adverbs are

a some adverbs of manner
b some adverbs of time

▷ 24.4 (adverbs with the same form as adjectives)

3 We form some adverbs from an adjective + **-ly**. These adverbs are

a most adverbs of manner ▷ 24.3
b some adverbs of frequency ▷ 24.11
c some adverbs of degree ▷ 24.12
d most adverbs referring to a whole sentence ▷ 24.13

▷ 30.3,6 (spelling)

4 We cannot form an adverb from an adjective which ends in **-ly**. Instead we can use

a **in a . . . way/manner** or
b an adverb of similar meaning

24.3 ADVERBS OF MANNER

1	**Adjective:**	The journey was very **slow**.
	Adverb:	We travelled **slowly**.
2	**Adjective:**	Mr Harris is a **careful** driver.
	Adverb:	He drives his car very **carefully**.
3	**Adjective:**	The climb up the hill was **easy**.
	Adverb:	We **easily** climbed the hill.

1 An adjective (e.g. *slow*) describes a noun (e.g. *journey*). An adverb of manner (e.g. *slowly*) describes a verb (e.g. *travelled*).

1,2,3 An adverb of manner ends in **-ly**. But ▷ 24.2,4; 24.8 (*well*)
2 An adverb of manner usually comes at the end of a sentence. It never comes between the verb and the direct object. ▷ 24.9
3 An adverb of manner sometimes has mid position.

▷ 30.3,6 (spelling)

24.4 ADVERBS WITH THE SAME FORM AS ADJECTIVES

1	**Adjective:**	Mrs Wells is a **hard** worker.
	Adverb:	She works very **hard**.
2	**Adjective:**	She was very **early** this morning.
	Adverb:	She started work **early**.
3	**Adjective:**	The **daily** newspaper arrives at seven o'clock.
	Adverb:	The newspaper arrives **daily** at seven o'clock.

1,2 **Hard** and **early** are both adjectives and adverbs.

Other adverbs with the same form as adjectives are **fast, high, low, deep, near, far, late** and **long**. But ▷ 24.5

3 **Daily, hourly, weekly, monthly** and **yearly** are both adjectives and adverbs. We form them from the nouns **day, hour** etc.

24.5 *HIGH, HIGHLY; NEAR, NEARLY; HARD, HARDLY; LATE, LATELY; MOST, MOSTLY*

1a The plane didn't fly very **high**.
b I read a **highly** amusing book on the plane.

2a Some birds came quite **near**.
b The plane **nearly** hit them.

3a The stewardesses worked very **hard**.
b They **hardly** had any time to sit down.

4a We arrived **late** because of bad weather.
b There have been a lot of storms **lately**.

5a What I hate **most** about air travel is waiting at airports.
b On long journeys I **mostly** travel by plane.

High, near, hard and **late** are adverbs with the same form as adjectives. ▷ 24.4 **Most** is an adverb with the same form as a quantifier. ▷ 20.16
Highly, nearly, hardly, lately and **mostly** are also adverbs, but they have different meanings from **high, near** etc.

1 **highly** = very
2 **nearly** = almost
3 **hardly** = almost no
4 **lately** = recently, not long ago
5 **mostly** = mainly, usually

24.6 ADJECTIVES AFTER *LOOK, SMELL* ETC

I feel **hungry**. (I **am** hungry.)
This dinner looks **nice**. (This dinner **is** nice.)
It smells **lovely**. (It's lovely.)
It tastes **delicious**. (It's delicious.)

We use an adjective (not an adverb) when we can use **be** instead of the verb.

We use an adjective after **feel, look, smell, taste, sound, seem, appear, become, get** (= become) and **stay**.

24.7 THE REGULAR COMPARISON OF ADVERBS

1 Eric Swift drove his car very **fast**. He went **faster** than the other drivers. He drove the **fastest**.

2 Linda's horse jumped **successfully**. It jumped over the fences **more successfully** than the other horses did. Her horse jumped the **most successfully**.

3 Eric went the **fastest** in the race.
Of all the horses, Linda's jumped **most successfully**.

1 Adverbs with the same form as adjectives (▷ 24.4) form their comparative and superlative with **-er** and **-est**.

2 Adverbs in **-ly** form their comparative and superlative with **more** and **most**.

3 The superlative of adverbs can be with or without **the**.

NOTE In the comparative and superlative we often use **be** and an adjective instead of a verb and an adverb, e.g. *He was faster than the other drivers. Her horse was the most successful.* ▷ 23.2

24.8 THE IRREGULAR COMPARISON OF ADVERBS

1 William is good at drawing. He can draw very **well**. He can draw **better** than Jill. She likes making models **best**.

2 The team had a bad game. They played **badly**. They played **worse** than last week. Jones played the **worst**.

3 Bob can swim a long way, but Martin can't swim very **far**. Debbie can swim **further/farther** than Martin, but Sarah can swim the **furthest**/the **farthest** of all.

Form

1 **well**	**better**	**best**
2 **badly**	**worse**	**worst**
3 **far**	**further/farther**	**furthest/farthest**

1 **Good** is an adjective; **well** is an adverb.

2 **Bad** is an adjective; **badly** is an adverb.

3 **Far** is an adjective and an adverb.

We use **far** in negative sentences and questions. We use **a long way** in positive sentences.

▷ 23.3 (irregular comparison of adjectives); 23.8 (*further/farther*)

24.9 THE POSITION OF ADVERBS

1 Front position

	Adverb	Subject + Verb	
a	**Yesterday**	the team played	well.
b	**Usually**	I go	to the café.
c	**Perhaps**	I'll see	you later.

There are three places in the sentence where adverbs can come.

1 **Front position** is at the beginning of the sentence.

In front position we put

a sometimes adverbs or adverb phrases of time and place ▷ 24.10
b sometimes adverbs of frequency ▷ 24.11
c sometimes adverbs referring to a whole sentence ▷ 24.13

▷ 28.2 (front position for emphasis)

2 Mid position

	Subject	(Auxiliary or modal verb)	Adverb	(Verb)	
a	He		**slowly**	opened	the door.
b	I		**usually**	go	to the café.
c	I	don't	**really**	like	fish.
d	We	've	**just**	finished	the job.
e	The story	is	**certainly**		very exciting.

2 **Mid position** is
a,b before a verb in the simple present or simple past tense
c,d after the first auxiliary or modal verb in the verb phrase
e after **be**

In mid position we put

a sometimes adverbs of manner ▷ 24.3
b adverbs of frequency ▷ 24.11
c some adverbs of degree ▷ 24.12
d sometimes a few adverbs of time ▷ 24.10
e sometimes adverbs referring to a whole sentence ▷ 24.13

3 End position

	Subject + Verb	(Direct object)	Adverbs and other phrases
a	The men talked		**quietly**.
b	He opened	the door	**slowly**.
c	The team played		**well at Nottingham yesterday**.
d	Eric danced		**a lot** with Mary.
e	He didn't dance		with his girlfriend **much**.
f	I go		to the café **usually**.
g	I'll see	you	later, **perhaps**.
h	We handed	the bottle	**carefully** to the policeman.
i	We handed	the bottle	to the policeman **today**.

3 **End position** is

a after the verb (if there is no direct object)

b after the verb + direct object

Sometimes there is more than one adverb or phrase in end position.

c The normal order is manner (e.g. *well*) + place (e.g. *at Nottingham*) + time (e.g. *yesterday*). ▷ 24.10

d We often put a short phrase (e.g. *a lot*) before a longer phrase (e.g. *with Mary*).

e Putting a word or phrase at the end of a sentence (e.g. *much*) makes it more important.

f In end position an adverb of frequency usually comes after an adverb or adverb phrase of place.

g An adverb referring to a whole sentence usually comes at the end of the sentence, sometimes after a comma.

h An adverb of manner often comes before an indirect object with **to**.

i An adverb or adverb phrase of time or place usually comes after an indirect object with **to**.

In end position we put

a,b,c,h	adverbs of manner ▷ 24.3
c,i	sometimes adverbs or adverb phrases of time and place ▷ 24.10
d,e	some adverbs of degree ▷ 24.12
f	sometimes adverbs of frequency ▷ 24.11
g	sometimes adverbs referring to a whole sentence ▷ 24.13

24.10 PLACE AND TIME

1a **At the disco** they played my favourite records.
b **Yesterday** they played my favourite records.
c They played my favourite records **at the disco**.
d They played my favourite records **yesterday**.

2a They played my favourite records **at the disco yesterday**.
b We went **there on Saturday evening**.

3a Bob will **soon** be here.
b He's **just** arrived.

1 An adverb or adverb phrase of place or of time can come at the beginning or end of a sentence.
2 Place comes before time in end position. ▷ 24.9
3 A few adverbs of time can have mid position, e.g. *soon, just, already, now, then.*

▷ 24.14 (*yet* and *still*)

24.11 ADVERBS OF FREQUENCY

1a My brother **always** stays in bed on Sunday morning.
b Do you **often** get up early? Have you **ever** got up at four o'clock?
c We can **never** wake Eric. He won't **normally** get up until twelve.
d I'm **sometimes** very tired on Sundays, too. I **usually** stay in bed a bit.

2a **Sometimes**, I don't get up at all on Sundays, but **usually** I'm up at nine.
b My father lies in bed until one o'clock **sometimes**. He's tired **usually**.
c Does he work late **often**?

Adverbs of frequency say **how often** something happens.

1 Adverbs of frequency have mid position. ▷ 24.9
2 a,b **Sometimes, usually** and **normally** can also have front or end position. ▷ 24.9
c **Often** can also have end position.

▷ 2.7 (the present continuous tense with *always*)

24.12 ADVERBS OF DEGREE

Describing adjectives and adverbs

1a This record's **rather** nice, but the music's **a bit** loud, isn't it?
b Sarah doesn't dance **very** often, but she dances **so** beautifully.
2 Is the music loud **enough**? – It's **too** loud.
3a £20 is **very**/**extremely** expensive for a meal.
b £12 is **rather**/**pretty**/**fairly**/**quite** expensive.
c £8 is **a bit**/**a little** expensive.
4 The food is **quite**/**absolutely** excellent.

Adverbs of degree make the meaning of an adjective or adverb **stronger** or **weaker**.

1 An adverb that describes an adjective or adverb comes before it.

2 But **enough** as an adverb of degree comes after the adjective or adverb that it describes.

3 **Very** and **extremely** make the meaning of an adjective or adverb stronger; **rather, pretty, fairly** and **quite** make the meaning a little stronger; and **a bit** and **a little** make the meaning weaker.

4 We also use **quite** to give emphasis to the meaning when the adjective or adverb already has a very strong meaning, e.g. *excellent* (= very good), *awful* (= very bad), *correct, sure.*

Describing verbs

5a I **just** love this record.
b I **rather** like it, too. I **almost** decided to buy it yesterday.

6 I didn't like their first record very **much**, but I like this one **a lot**.

Adverbs of degree can also make the meaning of a verb **stronger** or **weaker**.

5 An adverb of degree that describes a verb has mid position, e.g. *just, rather, almost.* ▷ 24.9

6 But **much, a lot, a bit** and **a little** have end position when they describe a verb. ▷ 24.9

24.13 ADVERBS REFERRING TO A WHOLE SENTENCE

Fortunately the weather looks nice.

Of course we can go.

Jane is **certainly** coming.

David will **probably** be here.

He won't be here, **actually**.

He can't come, **unfortunately**.

These adverbs show what the speaker thinks about the sentence. **Fortunately** means that the speaker is pleased that the weather looks nice.

Adverbs referring to a whole sentence can have front position, mid position or end position. ▷ 24.9

Other adverbs referring to a whole sentence:
in fact, really, surely, obviously, possibly, maybe, perhaps, naturally, (un)luckily.

▷ 33.4 (Communication: being sure and unsure)

24.14 *YET* AND *STILL*

1	Has the letter come **yet**? – No, it hasn't come **yet**.
2a	Are you **still** waiting for the letter? – Yes, I'm **still** waiting for it.
b	The letter **still** hasn't come./The letter has **still** not come.
c	It **still** isn't here./It's **still** not here.

1 We use **yet** to talk about something that we are waiting for.
We use **yet** in questions and in negative sentences.
Yet comes at the end of the sentence.

2 We use **still** to talk about something that is going on and is not finished.

Still comes
a in mid position in questions and positive sentences.
b,c before the auxiliary or modal verb + **n't** or between the auxiliary or modal verb and **not** in negative sentences.

24.15 *ONLY* AND *EVEN*

	Normal use
1	We **only** stayed one night at the hotel because we had to leave the next day.
2a	We **even** stayed four nights at the hotel because we liked it so much.
b	We could **only** get breakfast. We couldn't **even** get dinner.
3a	**Only** the food was nice. The room was awful.
b	**Even** the food was nice. The whole place was lovely.
4	The **only** food we could get at the pub was a cheese sandwich.
	Formal and official use
5	Mr and Mrs Fraser stayed **only** one night at the hotel.
6a	Ladies **only**.
b	This car park is for hotel guests **only**.

1 In informal spoken and written English, **only** has mid position. It need not come next to the word that it refers to, e.g. *one*.

2 **Even** also has mid position.

3 When **only** and **even** refer to the subject, they come before it.

4 We can also use **only** as an adjective.

5 In rather formal English, **only** can come before the word or phrase that it refers to, e.g. *one*.

6 In official written English, e.g. on notices, **only** comes after the word or phrase that it refers to, e.g. *ladies, hotel guests*.

25 Prepositions

25.1 PREPOSITIONS OF PLACE AND MOVEMENT

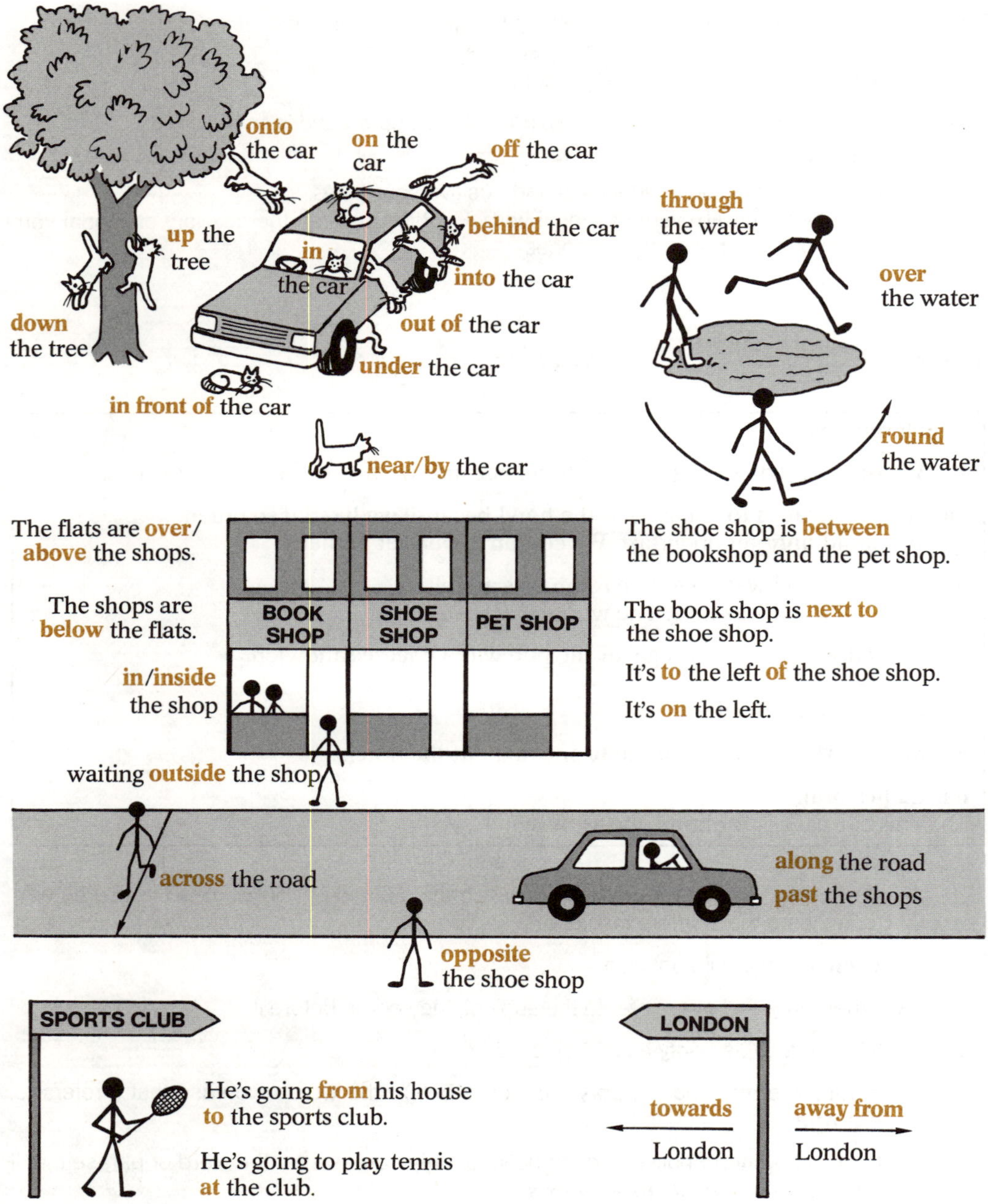

25.2 PREPOSITIONS OF PLACE: *AT* AND *IN*

a Simon was **at** the bus stop.	a Susan was **in** the garden.
b We live **at** 23 Bolton Road.	b We live **in** Bolton Road.
c The girls are **at** the cinema. (= ... watching a film.)	c It was dark **in** the cinema. (= ... inside the cinema.)
d The boys are **at** the swimming-pool. (= ... swimming or watching the swimmers.)	d It was cold **in** the swimming-pool. (= ... in the water.)
e We stopped **at** a village near Coventry.	e There were two shops **in** the village.
f The Jamesons live **at** Oxford.	f The Jamesons live **in** Oxford.
	g They're on holiday **in** Spain.

We use **at** with	We use **in** (= inside) with
a a position	a something big enough to be all around a person
b a house or an address	b a road or street
c,d a place for doing things	c,d a building or other large space
e a village or town on a journey	e a village
f a village or town (but **in** is more usual)	f a town or city
	g a country

25.3 PREPOSITIONS OF TIME: *AT, ON* AND *IN*

at

at four o'clock; **at** breakfast; **at** sunset; **at** Christmas; **at** the weekend; **at** that time

on

on Friday(s); **on** May 21st; **on** the next day

in

in the morning; **in** June; **in** summer; **in** 1985

No preposition

Are you going to the film **this week**? – No, **next Tuesday**. – We saw it **last year**.

In informal American English the preposition is also left out in e.g. *He'll be back Saturday. There's no one here mornings.*

▷ 19.6 (phrases of time without *the*)

25.4 PREPOSITIONS OF TIME: *BEFORE, DURING* AND *AFTER*

The post office is very busy **before** Christmas.
It's difficult to travel **during** a public holiday.
We had to take a taxi home **after** the party.

We can also use **before** and **after** as conjunctions. ▷ 15.2; 27.2
During is a preposition; **while** is a conjunction with the same meaning. ▷ 15.2; 17.2; 27.2

25.5 PREPOSITIONS OF TIME: *TILL/UNTIL* AND *BY*

1 Can I keep this book **till** Friday/**until** Friday, please?
2 Yes, but I'd like it back **by** the weekend.

Till Friday/**until** Friday = from now to Friday.
Till is more informal than **until**.

By the weekend = not later than the weekend

▷ 27.2 (*till/until* as a conjunction)

25.6 PREPOSITIONS OF TIME: *FROM ... TO/TILL/UNTIL*

The sale was **from** December 28th **to** January 3rd.
The shop is open **from** nine **till** five thirty.
It will be closed **from** tomorrow **until** next Tuesday.

We use **from ... to/till/until** to talk about the beginning and end of a period of time.

25.7 PREPOSITIONS OF TIME: *FOR, SINCE* AND *AGO*

1 Dick hasn't been here **for** six months.
2 We haven't seen him **since** March.
3 We last saw him six months **ago**.

1 Mary hasn't telephoned **for** three weeks.
2 We haven't heard from her **since** then.
3 I last heard from her three weeks **ago**.

1 We use **for** to talk about a period of time, e.g. *six months, three weeks.*
2 We use **since** to talk about a point of time, e.g. *March, then.*
3 We use **ago** (= before now) to talk about a point of past time, seen from the present.

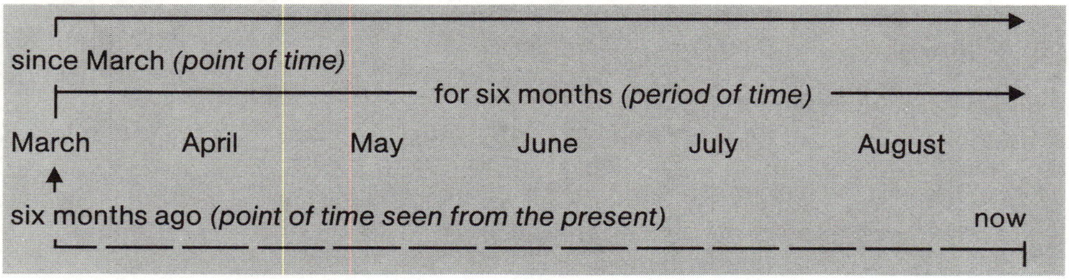

▷ 3.4, 8, 9 (*for* and *since* with perfect tenses); 15.2; 27.2 (*since* as a conjunction)

25.8 MEANS OF TRANSPORT AND COMMUNICATION: *BY*

How did you get here? –
I came **by** bicycle/**by** bus/**by** train/**by** car/**by** taxi/**by** sea/**by** boat/**by** air/**by** plane.
But: I walked./I came **on** foot.
How can we let your friends know? –
By letter./**By** telegram./**By** telephone.

25.9 MEANS: *WITH* AND *BY*

How did the thief get in?

1 He opened the door **with** a key.
2 He got in **by** using a key.

1 We use **with** to talk about the **means** or **instrument** of an action. But ▷ 25.8
2 We use **by** before an -ing form. ▷ 15.2

26 Verbs with adverbs and prepositions

26.1 PHRASAL VERBS

1 We **went away** for two weeks. We only **came back** yesterday.
2 I'm sure I **wrote down** the address, but I think I **threw away** the piece of paper.
3 The plan didn't **come off** – I'm afraid it **fell through**.
4 Mr Gray doesn't want to **give up** smoking, but he's **cutting down** the numbers of cigarettes he smokes.

A phrasal verb is a verb + adverb, e.g. *go away.*

1,2 Sometimes the meaning of a phrasal verb is clear from the meaning of the verb and adverb, e.g. *go away, come back, write down, throw away.*
3,4 Sometimes the verb + adverb has a special meaning, e.g. *come off* (= succeed), *fall through* (= not succeed), *give up* (= stop), *cut down* (= reduce).

1,3 These phrasal verbs have no object.
2,4 These phrasal verbs have an object, e.g. *wrote down the address.*

26.2 PHRASAL VERBS WITH AN OBJECT

1a The young people **picked up** the litter.
b The young people **picked** the litter **up**.

2a A lorry **took away** all the bottles.
b A lorry **took** all the bottles **away**.

3 The young people **picked up** the litter left by the crowd.
A lorry **took away** all the bottles they found.

4 What about the litter? – The young people **picked** it **up**.
Who took the bottles? – A lorry **took** them **away**.

1,2 If the object of a phrasal verb is a noun, the adverb can come
a before the object or
b after it.

3 If the object is **very long** (e.g. *the litter left by the crowd*), then the adverb comes in front of it.

4 If the object is a **pronoun**, the adverb always comes after it.

26.3 PREPOSITIONAL VERBS

We finally **decided on** a holiday in Morocco.

We had to **wait for** the plane.

Can I **look at** your photos?

A prepositional verb is a verb + preposition, e.g. *decide on.*
The preposition comes before the object of a prepositional verb, e.g. *decide on a holiday.*

Other prepositional verbs are **listen to, ask for, pay for, look for, look after, hope for** and **deal with**. And ▷ 15.4

26.4 PHRASAL VERBS AND PREPOSITIONAL VERBS

1	**Phrasal verb:**	The students **looked** the words **up**.
	Phrasal verb:	The students **looked up** the words.
	Phrasal verb:	The words **were looked up**.
2	**Prepositional verb:**	The students **looked at** the text. [ət]
	Prepositional verb:	The text **was looked at.** [æt]

1 We can stress the adverb: ′looked ′up

2 We cannot stress the preposition: ′looked at. (unless we want to give it extra emphasis ▷ 28.1)

26.5 PHRASAL-PREPOSITIONAL VERBS

I say we should **do away with** the House of Lords.

Let's hurry up and **get on with** the job.

I hope you won't **go back on** your promise now.

I can't **keep up with** that sports car; it's going too fast.

Don't **let** Mr Barnes **in on** our secret!

I'm really **looking forward to** the holidays.

Do high wages **make up for** poor working conditions?

Why do you **put up with** all this noise?

I've **sent away for** the free map in this advertisement.

Watch out for cows in the road here!

A phrasal-prepositional verb is a verb + adverb + preposition, e.g. *do away with.*

do away with = get rid of
get on with = do (a job) immediately, without waiting
go back on = break (a promise)
keep up with = go as fast as
let (someone) in on = tell (someone) a secret
look forward to = think of (something in the future) with pleasure
make up for = be so good that (something unpleasant) seems less important
put up with = not complain about (something unpleasant)
send away for = write a letter to ask for (something in an advertisement)
watch out for = look carefully for

26.6 NOUNS FORMED FROM PHRASAL VERBS

1a I'd like to lie down.
b I'd like a **lie-down**.

2a Someone broke in last night.
b There was a **break-in** last night.

3a I'm going to clean this room out.
b I'm going to give this room a **clean-out**.

4a The prisoners got away at night.
b They made their **getaway** at night.

We can change some phrasal verbs (a) into nouns (b).

Most nouns formed from phrasal verbs have a hyphen (–). ▷ 37.6 But see 4b.

27 Conjunctions and other linking words

27.1 MAIN CLAUSES AND SUB CLAUSES

Two main clauses

1 I've got a headache, and I feel sick.

Sub clauses with *if, when, because* etc

2a We can go if you like.
b If you like, we can go.

a We'll go when this film's over.
b When this film's over, we'll go.

Reported clauses

3a It said in the paper (that) it finishes at ten.
b It finishes at ten, it said in the paper.

Relative clauses

4a The film that came first was awful.
b 'Love in the East', which came first, was awful.

Conjunctions

1 We join two main clauses together with the conjunctions **and, but** and **or**.
2 A sub clause (e.g. an if-clause or a clause of time) begins with a conjunction, e.g. **if, when, because, so that**.
3 A reported clause begins with **that** or has no conjunction. ▷ 12.1 For reported questions ▷ 12.5
4 A relative clause begins with a relative pronoun. ▷ 22.1 But ▷ 22.4

Order of clauses

2 A sub clause with **if, when, because** etc can come before or after the main clause.
3 A reported clause usually comes after the main clause.
4 A relative clause comes after the noun it tells us about.

Pauses and commas

1 We sometimes put a comma between two main clauses. ▷ 37.3
2,3 If the main clause comes first (a), there is no need for a pause (in speech) or a comma (in writing).
If the sub clause or reported clause comes first (b), there is a pause or comma after it.
4 We do not use pauses or commas with a defining relative clause (a).
A non-defining relative clause (b) has pauses and commas before and after it. ▷ 22.12

▷ 37.3 (punctuation)

27.2 CLAUSES OF TIME

It started to rain **when/while/as** I was working in the garden.
I wanted to plant a few things **before** it rained.
After/When/As soon as I'd cut the grass, the rain came down.
I'll stay inside **till/until** it stops.
We haven't had any rain **since** we came back from our holidays.

Clauses of time can come either before or after the main clause. ▷ 27.1

▷ 15.2 (the -ing form); 17.2 (the -ing form)

27.3 CLAUSES WITH *AND, TOO, AS WELL* AND *ALSO*

1 Harry rides a motor-bike, **and** he can drive a car (, **too/as well**).
2 Harry rides a motor-bike. He can **also** drive a car.
3 David likes modern jazz **as well as** pop music.
4 David likes **both** pop music **and** modern jazz.
5 Jean is **not only** a good singer, (**but**) she **also** plays the guitar.

1 When **and** links two clauses, it comes at the beginning of the second clause. We can also use **too** or **as well** at the end of the second clause.
2 **Also** has mid position, but it can have front or end position or come after the first phrase in the sentence.
3 **As well as** is emphatic.
4 **Both ... and** is emphatic.
5 **Not only ... (but) also** is emphatic.

▷ 9.1 (short additions to statements)

27.4 GIVING ALTERNATIVES

1 We can buy a colour television **or** a black and white one.
2a We can buy **either** a colour television **or** a black and white one.
b We can **either** buy a television **or** hire one.
3a There isn't any sport today on BBC **or** on ITV/**either** on BBC **or** on ITV.
b I don't think **either of them** is/are showing any sport.
4a **Neither** BBC **nor** ITV is/are showing any sport.
b **Neither of them** is/are showing any sport.

1 We use **or** to talk about an alternative.
2 **Either ... or** is emphatic. Each word comes before an alternative.
3 We can also use **either** and **or** with a negative verb.
4 **Neither** and **nor** have a negative meaning.

We use **either** and **neither** to talk about **two** things. ▷ 20.20 *(both)*

▷ 8.2 (alternative questions)

27.5 CLAUSES OF CONTRAST: *WHEREAS, WHILE* AND *ON THE OTHER HAND*

1 America is a rich country, **whereas**/**while** India is a poor country.

2 America is an industrial country. India, **on the other hand**, has hardly any industry.

1 **Whereas** and **while** come at the beginning of a clause.
2 **On the other hand** often has mid position or comes after the first phrase in the sentence, but it can have front or end position.

27.6 CLAUSES OF CONTRAST: *BUT, HOWEVER* ETC

1 Thousands of pupils are leaving school, **but** there are no jobs for them.

2 Thousands of pupils are leaving school. There are, **however**, no jobs for them.

3a **Although**/**Even though** Ann did well at school, she can't find a job.
b Ann can't find a job **although**/**even though** she did well at school.

4a **In spite of** doing well at school, Ann can't find a job.
b Ann can't find a job **in spite of** doing well at school.

1 **But** comes at the beginning of a clause.

2 **However** often has mid position or comes after the first phrase in the sentence, but it can have front or end position.

3,4 Clauses with **although, even though** and **in spite of** can come either before or after the main clause.

▷ 15.2 (the -ing form); 17.5 (the -ed form)

27.7 CLAUSES OF REASON

Why weren't the trains running?
Most trains weren't running **because of** the weather.
They were not running **because** it was snowing heavily.
We decided not to travel **as**/**since** so many trains were not running.

Because of the weather, most trains weren't running.
Because it was snowing heavily, they were not running.
As/**Since** so many trains were not running, we decided not to travel.

Phrases with **because of** and clauses with **because, as** and **since** can come either before or after the main clause.

▷ 17.4 (the -ing form and the -ed form)

27.8 CLAUSES OF PURPOSE

Why has the government put up taxes?

It has put up taxes **to** get more money from us.

It needs more money **in order to** build more schools.

The teachers called a parents' meeting **so as to** hear everyone's opinion.

They're building a school here **so that** pupils will not need to travel so far in future.

Schools are **for** learning. ▷ 15.2

The phrase or clause of purpose comes after the main clause.

In order to and **so as to** are rather formal.
In a clause with **so that** we often use **can, could, will, would** or **needn't**.

27.9 CLAUSES OF RESULT: *SO, THEREFORE* ETC

1 Last year's team manager was no good, (and) **so** he had to leave.
2 The new manager is much better, and the team is **therefore** happier.
3 He's bought two new players, and **as a result**, the whole team is playing better.
4 The team have won their last four games easily. **Consequently**, more people are coming to watch them.

1 **(And) so** always comes at the beginning of a clause, but it does not normally start a new sentence.
2 **Therefore** often has mid position, but it can have front or end position.
3-4 **As a result** and **consequently** often have front position or come after the first phrase in the sentence, but they can have mid or end position.

2-4 We can use **therefore, as a result** and **consequently** in a clause with **and** (e.g. *and as a result, ...*) or in a new sentence (e.g. *Consequently, ...*).

27.10 CLAUSES OF RESULT: *SO/SUCH ... (THAT)*

This coffee's **so** nice **that** I'm going to have another cup.

I've eaten **so** much I can't stand up.

It's **such** an expensive restaurant **that** we can't come here very often.

We've had **such** lovely food here I won't forget it for a long time.

We can leave out **that** in informal speech.

27.11 CONDITIONAL CLAUSES

I shall go to the dinner **if** I get an invitation. –
Well, I shall go **even if** nobody asks me. –
But you won't be able to go **unless** you're invited. –
I'm going **if/whether** I'm invited or not. **As long as** it isn't next Friday, I'll be there. –
We'll be going **provided (that)** our car is all right.

Unless = if … not
These clauses can come either before or after the main clause.
▷ 11 (if-clauses); 27.1 (main clauses and sub clauses)

27.12 COMPOUNDS WITH *-EVER*

Whenever I do a maths problem, I get the wrong answer.
(= Every time I do a maths problem …)
I'd do better if I wrote **whatever** number comes into my head.
(= … any number that comes into my head.)
However hard I try, I can't understand maths.
(= It doesn't matter how hard I try …)

In the words **whenever, whatever, however, whoever, whichever** and **wherever,** the meaning of **-ever** is **every, any** or **it doesn't matter.** ▷ 20.13
We also use **however** to express contrast. ▷ 27.6

27.13 GIVING EXAMPLES

There are lots of big cities in America **such as** New York and Los Angeles.
Many Blacks live in ghettos **like** Harlem.
Thousands of Europeans went to live in the USA – British, Germans and Italians, **for example**.
Some cities have financial problems, **e.g.** New York.

28 Emphasis

28.1 EMPHATIC STRESS

1 The party's on *Fri*day. (not on Saturday)
2 Is *John* going with you? (not Brian)

When we want to give emphasis to a word or phrase (make it more important), we can give it extra stress. ▷ Glossary; 39.1
The voice falls (1) or rises (2) on the word with emphatic stress.

28.2 EMPHATIC WORD ORDER

1 **'Eatwell'** the restaurant was called.
2 The steak was nice, but **this pudding** I don't like at all.
3 **Slowly** the restaurant began to fill up.

If we want to give emphasis to a word or phrase, we can put it at the beginning of the clause or sentence.

We can do this with
1 a complement ▷ 1.1
2 an object
3 an adverb ▷ 28.7

▷ 10.1 (use of the passive)

28.3 *IT + BE* USED FOR EMPHASIS

1a *Your friend* took us to York.
b **It was your friend who** took us to York.

2a *York* has a city wall, hasn't it?
b **It's York that** has a city wall, isn't it?

3a We went to York *last August*.
b **It was last August that** we went to York.

4a We went with *Bob*.
b **It was Bob** we went with.

5a *I* wanted to see the railway museum.
b **It was me that** wanted to see the railway museum.

1,2 We can use **it + be** and a relative clause to give emphasis to a word or phrase, e.g. *your friend, York.*
3 We can also use **it + be** to give emphasis to an adverb or adverb phrase, e.g. *last August.*
4 We can leave out **who** or **that** when it is the object of the relative clause or when there is a preposition. ▷ 22.4
5 If we use a pronoun after **it + be**, we use the object form, e.g. *me.* ▷ 20.1

28.4 *WHAT* USED FOR EMPHASIS

I need *a good sleep*.
What I need is a good sleep.

I'm going to *go to bed*.
What I'm going to do is go to bed.

We can use **what** + clause + **be** to give emphasis to a word or phrase.
What = the thing that

▷ 22.9 (*what* in relative clauses)

28.5 EMPHATIC PRONOUNS

1a Did *you* build this new wall?
b Did you build this new wall **yourself**?

2a *The house* is very old.
b The house **itself** is very old.

Form The emphatic pronouns have the same form as the reflexive pronouns. ▷ 20.7
The emphatic pronoun has end position *(you ... yourself)* or it comes after the noun phrase it refers to *(the house itself)*.

Use We use emphatic pronouns (b) to give emphasis to a noun phrase, e.g. *you, the house.*

▷ 20.8

28.6 THE EMPHATIC FORM OF THE VERB

1a These motorways aren't necessary.
b But I think they *'are* necessary.
2a They shouldn't build them.
b I think they *'should* build them.
3a People don't use them.
b But people *'do* use them.
4a You didn't come on the motorway.
b I *'did* come on the motorway.

We use the emphatic form of the verb (b) to give emphasis to the meaning of a whole sentence.

1,2 Auxiliary and modal verbs are stressed in the emphatic form.
3,4 The simple present and simple past tenses have an emphatic form with **do**. The form of **do** is stressed. ▷ 5.8

▷ 6 (the imperative and *let's)*

28.7 EMPHATIC USE OF *HERE* AND *THERE*

1a The bus is late. - **Here it comes** now, look.
b **Here comes the bus**.
2a Where are the children? – **There they are**.
b **There are the children**, over there.

Form We can put **here** or **there** at the beginning of a sentence.
The verb is the present tense of **be** or a verb in the simple present tense (usually **come** or **go**).
If the subject is a pronoun, it comes before the verb (e.g. *Here* it *comes*). If the subject is a noun, it comes after the verb (*Here comes* the bus).

Use We use **here** and **there** at the beginning of a sentence to draw someone's attention to (= make someone look at) something that we can see.

29 Word-building

29.1 NOUNS FOR JOBS AND OTHER ACTIVITIES

-er/-or

teach**er**, build**er**, wait**er**, manag**er**, driv**er**
doct**or**, edit**or**, act**or**

-ist ▷ 29.5
art**ist**, chem**ist**, journal**ist**, tour**ist**

-ant/-ent
shop assist**ant**, civil serv**ant**, account**ant**
travel ag**ent**, stud**ent**, presid**ent**

-man/-woman/-person

police**man**, post**man**, milk**man**, sales**man**, chair**man**
police**woman**, post**woman**
sales**person** (= salesman or saleswoman), chair**person**

-ess

actr**ess**, waitr**ess**, princ**ess**

Words in **-man** refer to men; words in **-woman** or **-ess** refer to women; other words refer to both men and women, e.g. *teacher, doctor, student.* But we can say e.g. **a woman teacher, women doctors, a male nurse, a female student.**

29.2 COMPOUND NOUNS

a **shoe shop**	= a shop that sells shoes
film stars	= stars who are in films
a **police-car**	= a car that belongs to the police
a **bus driver**	= a person who drives a bus
a **bedroom**	= a room with a bed

In most compound nouns, the main stress is on the first noun, e.g. ′shoe shop.

The first noun in the compound is always singular, e.g. shoe *shop* (a shop that sells shoe**s**). Plural: **shoe shops**.

Other compound nouns: **bank robber, girlfriend, housework, pocket-money, birthday card, headache, youth club, matchbox, toy factory**. And ▷ 29.3

▷ 23.11 (nouns used as adjectives); 37.6 (the hyphen)

29.3 COMPOUND NOUNS WITH ADJECTIVES AND -ING FORMS

1 Mr Smith was in his ′**greenhouse**.
(= a building for growing plants in)

2 Mr Smith lives in the **green ′house**.
(= the house which is green)

1 We sat in the ′**waiting room**.
(= the room for waiting in)

2 The police controlled the **waiting ′crowds**.
(= the crowds who were waiting)

1 **Greenhouse** and **waiting room** are compound nouns. The stress (′) is on the first part of the compound.

Other compound nouns: **high school, sweet shop, grandfather; drinking water, riding lesson, playing-field, washing-machine, shopping bag**. And ▷ 29.2

▷ 37.6 (the hyphen)

2 **Green house** and **waiting crowds** are both adjective + noun (▷ 17.1; 23.1). The stress is on the noun.

29.4 NOUNS FORMED FROM VERBS

1 give → **giving**, make → **making** etc

The new university is going to be built. This will begin next month.
The **building** of the new university will begin next month.

2 attack → **attack**, change → **change** etc

The government has promised more money for schools. This has pleased teachers.
The **promise** of more money for schools has pleased teachers.

3 communicate → **communication**, suggest → **suggestion**, produce → **production** etc

Our economic problems were discussed. This was very interesting.
The **discussion** of our economic problems was very interesting.

4 move → **movement**, develop → **development** etc

The factory will employ 3,000 people. This will be a great help to the area.
The **employment** of 3,000 people will be a great help to the area.

Most nouns formed from verbs have **of** before the object (e.g. *the building* of *the new university*), but some nouns have other prepositions after them, e.g. *an attack* on *the government, a change* in/of *policy*.

▷ 26.6 (nouns formed from phrasal verbs)

29.5 *-ISM* AND *-IST*

We're talking about	social**ism**.	Mr X is	a social**ist**.
	commun**ism**.		a commun**ist**.
	racial**ism**.		a racial**ist**.
	national**ism**.		a national**ist**.
	conservat**ism**.	But:	a conservative.
	radical**ism**.		a radical
	liberal**ism**.		a liberal
	republican**ism**.		a republican
But:	Christianity		a Christian
	Islam		a Muslim

We use **-ism** to talk about a belief and **-ist** to talk about a person who believes in something.

▷ 19.8 (*a/an*); 29.1 (*-ist* for jobs)

29.6 OPPOSITES

Word pairs

long/short, easy/difficult, up/down, front/back

un-

unhappy, unwanted, unpack, unemployment, unfortunately

in-; **im-** (+ m/p); **ir-** (+ r); **il-** (+ l)

incomplete, **in**expensive; **im**moral, **im**possible; **ir**regular; **il**legal

dis-

dishonest, **dis**like, **dis**agree

29.7 COMPOUND ADJECTIVES

Noun/adverb + -ing form

Britain is an **oil-producing** country.
Reducing taxes is a **vote-winning** policy.
Are the British **hard-working** enough?

Adverb/adjective + -ed form

Mrs Johnson always looks **well-dressed**.
She's the **fair-haired** woman, isn't she?
She's got a very **badly-paid** job.

The noun in the compound is always singular, e.g. ***a** vote-**winning policy*** (= a policy that wins vote**s**). We use a hyphen (-) in compound adjectives.

▷ 17.1 (the -ing form and the -ed form used as adjectives)

29.8 COMPOUND ADJECTIVES WITH NUMBERS

Number + noun

The Goulds are a **two-car** family.
It's a **15-minute** drive to Glasgow.

Number + noun + adjective

Mr Gould is a **40-year-old** businessman.
There was a **three-foot-deep** hole in the road.

The noun in the compound is always singular, e.g. *a two-*car *family* (= a family with two car**s**).
We use a hyphen (–) in compound adjectives.
For *15 minutes' drive* ▷ 18.6

29.9 *OVER-* AND *UNDER-*

The houses and flats are **overcrowded** with people.
(= too crowded)

Most workers here are **underpaid**.
(= not paid enough)

More examples: **overwork, overeat; overpopulation; underused, underdeveloped, undercooked, underfed**.
We sometimes use a hyphen in these words. ▷ 37.6

29.10 *RE-*

The supermarket was **rebuilt** after the fire. (= built again)

They **re-opened** it last year. (= opened it again)

More examples: **rewrite, refill, remarry, recapture, retell, re-enter, re-use**.
▷ 37.6 (the hyphen)

29.11 *MIS-*

The children are **misbehaving** again. (= behaving badly)

I must have **miscounted** the money. (= counted wrongly)

More examples: **mishear, misunderstand, misinform, misuse, mismanage, misspell, mispronounce.**

30 The pronunciation and spelling of endings

30.1 THE PRONUNCIATION (SPEAKING) OF *-S/-ES*

1 shops	[ps]	2 sees	[i:z]	3 prices	[sɪz]
writes	[ts]	eyes	[aiz]	loses	[zɪz]
Jack's	[ks]	jobs	[bz]	watches	[tʃɪz]
cliffs	[fs]	beds	[dz]	Mr Blish's	[ʃɪz]

1 **-s** is [s] after voiceless sounds (but see note 3).

2 **-s** is [z] after voiced sounds (but see note 3).

3 **-s/-es** is [ɪz] after the sounds [s], [z], [ʃ], [ʒ], [tʃ] and [dʒ].

▷ Glossary *(voiced/voiceless)*; 2.4 (the simple present); 18.1, 2 (plurals of nouns), 18.4 (the possessive form)

30.2 PUTTING IN *E* BEFORE *-S*

1 dish → dishes	2 price → prices
box → boxes	lose → loses
watch → watches	realize → realizes

1 After the sounds [s], [z], [ʃ], [ʒ], [tʃ] and [dʒ] the ending is **-es**.

2 If the word ends in **e**, the ending is **-s**.

30.3 LEAVING OUT *E*

1 write → writing	3 make → makes
like → liked	nice → nicely
nice → nicer	4 true → truly
fine → finest	whole → wholly
2 agree — agreeing/agreed	5 possible → possibly
	probable → probably

1 We leave out **e** before an ending with a vowel, e.g. **-ing, -ed, -er, -est**.

2 If the **e** is part of a vowel sound (e.g. *agree*), we do not leave it out before **-ing**.

3 We do **not** leave out **e** before an ending with a consonant, e.g. **-s, -ly**.

4 But we leave out **e** from **true** and **whole** before **-ly**.

5 When an adjective ending in **-le** becomes an adverb, **e** changes to **y**.

30.4 THE PRONUNCIATION (SPEAKING) OF *-ED*

1	stopped	[pt]	2	showed	[əʊd]	3	waited	[tɪd]
	looked	[kt]		played	[eɪd]		ended	[dɪd]
	passed	[st]		cleaned	[nd]			
	laughed	[ft]		used	[zd]			

1 **-ed** is [t] after voiceless sounds (but see note 3).
2 **-ed** is [d] after voiced sounds (but see note 3).
3 **-ed** is [ɪd] after [t] and [d].

▷ Glossary *(voiced/voiceless)*; 3.3 (the simple past); 3.4 (the present perfect)

30.5 THE DOUBLING OF CONSONANTS

1	plan	pla**nn**ing	2	play	playing	3	be'gin	begi**nn**ing
	stop	sto**pp**ed		show	showed	4	'visit	visiting
	big	bi**gg**er		clean	cleaner	5	travel	trave**ll**ing
	fat	fa**tt**est		short	shortest			

1 In short words with one written vowel (**a, e, i, o, u**) + one written consonant (**n, p, g, t** etc), we double the consonant (**nn, pp, gg, tt**) before an ending with a vowel, e.g. **-ing, -ed, -er** or **-est**.
2 We do not double the consonant if it is **y** or **w** (e.g. *play, show*).
We do not double it if we write the vowel with two letters (e.g. *clean*).
We do not double it if the word ends in two written consonants (e.g. *short*) or in **x**.
3 In longer words we double the consonant if the last part of the word is stressed (e.g. *be'gin*).
4 We do **not** double the consonant if the last part of the word is unstressed (e.g. *'visit*).
5 But we double **l** in British English (e.g. GB *travelled*, USA *traveled*).

30.6 CONSONANT + *Y*

1	lady → lad**ie**s	2	the lad**y's** dress	3	play → played
	fly → fl**ie**s		the lad**ies'** dresses	4	fly → flying
	carry → carr**ie**d			5	lie → l**y**ing
	funny → funn**ie**r				
	silly → sill**ie**st				
	happy → happ**i**ly				

1 In words ending in a consonant (**d, l, r, n, p** etc) + **y**, the **y** changes to **ie** before **-s** and to **i** before **-ed, -er, -est** and **-ly**.
2 In the possessive form we use an apostrophe + **s** with a singular noun and an apostrophe with a plural noun. ▷ 18.4
3 **y** does **not** change after a vowel.
4 **y** does **not** change before **-ing**.
5 **ie** changes to **y** before **-ing**.

31 Numbers, money etc

31.1 CARDINAL NUMBERS

0	nought/zero						
1	one	11	**eleven**	21	twenty-one	101	a/one hundred and one
2	two	12	**twelve**	22	twenty-two		
3	three	13	**thir**teen	30	**thir**ty	138	a/one hundred and thirty-eight
4	four	14	fourteen	40	**for**ty		
5	five	15	**fif**teen	50	**fif**ty	572	five hundred and seventy-two
6	six	16	sixteen	60	sixty		
7	seven	17	seventeen	70	seventy	1,000	a/one thousand
8	eight	18	eighteen	80	eighty	36,429	thirty-six thousand four hundred and twenty-nine
9	nine	19	nineteen	90	ninety		
10	ten	20	**twen**ty	100	a/one hundred		
						1,000,000	a/one million

One thousand is written 1,000 or 1 000.

In Britain **one billion** = one million million *or* one thousand million

In America **one billion** = one thousand million

For 0 ▷ 31.5, 8

31.2 ORDINAL NUMBERS

1st	**first**	11th	eleventh	100th	hundredth/one hundredth
2nd	**second**	12th	**twelf**th	101st	(one) hundred and **first**
3rd	**third**	13th	thirteenth	133rd	(one) hundred and thirty-**third**
		20th	twent**ieth**		
4th	fourth	40th	fort**ieth**	157th	(one) hundred and fifty-seventh
5th	**fif**th	50th	fift**ieth**		
8th	eigh**t**h	86th	eighty-sixth	1,000th	(one) thousandth
9th	**nin**th	90th	ninet**ieth**		

Elizabeth II = Elizabeth the Second

31.3 *ONCE, TWICE* ETC

I clean my teeth **once** a day/**twice** a day/**three times** a day/**four times** a day/**five times** a day.

31.4 FRACTIONS

$\frac{1}{2}$	a/one **half**	$\frac{5}{8}$	five **eighths**	$5\frac{1}{4}$	five and a quarter
$\frac{1}{3}$	a/one **third**	$1\frac{1}{2}$	one and a half	$21\frac{7}{16}$	twenty-one and seven **sixteenths**
$\frac{3}{4}$	three **quarters**	$\frac{2}{3}$	two thirds		

31.5 DECIMALS

0.5	**point** five/nought **point** five/oh **point** five	
	zero **point** five *(USA)*	(= $\frac{1}{2}$)
2.33	two **point** three three	(= $2\frac{1}{3}$)
5.75	five **point** seven five	(= $5\frac{3}{4}$)

31.6 PERCENTAGES

50%	fifty **per cent** [pə'sent]
$2\frac{1}{2}$%	two and a half **per cent**
6.25%	six point two five **per cent**

31.7 SUMS

16 + 7 = 23	Sixteen **and** seven **is** twenty-three. Sixteen **plus** seven **equals** twenty-three.
18 − 5 = 13	Eighteen **take away** five **is** thirteen. Eighteen **minus** five **equals** thirteen.
4 × 9 = 36	Four nines **are** thirty-six. Four **times** nine **is** thirty-six. Four **multiplied by** nine **equals** thirty-six.
27 ÷ 3 = 9	Twenty-seven **divided by** three **is**/ **equals** nine.

31.8 TELEPHONE NUMBERS

0270 53399	**oh** two seven **oh**, five three three nine nine **oh** two seven **oh**, five **double** three **double** nine

31.9 MONEY

1p	a **penny**/one **p** [pi:]
10p	ten **pence**/ten **p**
£1	a **pound**/one **pound**
£3-75/£3.75	three **pound(s)** seventy-five **pence** three **pound(s)** seventy-five three seventy-five
1¢	a/one **cent**
$1	a/one **dollar**
$3.75	three **(dollars)** seventy-five **(cents)**

31.10 THE TIME OF DAY

7.00	seven o'clock/seven *(informal)*
8.00 am	eight am [eɪ'em] (= before noon)
3.25 pm	three twenty-five pm [piː'em] (= after noon)
7.30	half past seven/seven thirty/half seven *(informal)*
7.15	(a) quarter past seven/seven fifteen
7.45	(a) quarter to eight/seven forty-five
9.20	twenty (minutes) past nine/nine twenty
9.55	five (minutes) to ten/nine fifty-five
10.23	twenty-three minutes past ten/ten twenty-three
10.46	fourteen minutes to eleven/ten forty-six

We can leave out **o'clock** in informal speech, e.g. *I'll see you at seven.*
We can leave out **minutes** only after, 5, 10, 20 and 25, e.g. *twenty past nine* but *twenty-one* minutes *past nine.*
After and **of** are also used in American English instead of **past** and **to**, e.g. *twenty after nine, a quarter of eight.*
Times are sometimes written 7:00, 3:25 etc in American English.

31.11 DATES

23 June/23rd June	*(GB and USA)*	the twenty-third of June twenty-third June *(USA)*
June 23rd/June 23	*(GB and USA)*	June the twenty-third June twenty-third *(USA)*
1982		nineteen eighty-two

In Britain 1.4.82 = 1st April 1982
In America 1.4.82 = 4th January 1982

31.12 MEASUREMENTS

Kay is five **feet** six **inches** (5 ft 6 ins/5′6″)/a hundred and sixty-eight **centimetres** (168 cm) tall.

1 inch = 2.54 cm; 12 inches = 1 foot = 30.48 cm

One hundred **metres** (100 m) is further than one hundred **yards** (100 yds).

3 feet = 1 yard = 91.44 cm

It's five **miles**/eight **kilometres** (8 km) to the next town.

1760 yards = 1 mile = 1.61 km

I need four **ounces** (4 oz)/a hundred **grammes/grams** (100 gm) of flour.

1 ounce = 31.10 gm

Can I have four **pounds** (4 lbs)/two **kilos** (2 kg) of potatoes, please?

16 ounces = 1 pound = 0.454 kg

Mr Fraser drank a **pint**/half a **litre** of beer with the meal.

1 pint = 0.57 litres = 1.20 pints (USA)

We bought five **gallons**/twenty **litres** of petrol.

8 pints = 1 gallon = 4.54 litres = 1.20 gallons (USA)

The temperature in London is sixty-eight **degrees Fahrenheit** (68°F)/twenty **degrees Centigrade** (20°C).

31.13 THE ALPHABET

A [eɪ]	**E** [iː]	**I** [aɪ]	**M** [em]	**Q** [kjuː]	**U** [juː]	**Y** [waɪ]
B [biː]	**F** [ef]	**J** [dʒeɪ]	**N** [en]	**R** [ɑː]	**V** [viː]	**Z** [zed]/
C [siː]	**G** [dʒiː]	**K** [keɪ]	**O** [əʊ]	**S** [es]	**W** ['dʌbljuː]	[ziː]
D [diː]	**H** [eɪtʃ]	**L** [el]	**P** [piː]	**T** [tiː]	**X** [eks]	*(USA)*

32 Communication: Starting and finishing a conversation

32.1 STARTING A CONVERSATION WITH A STRANGER

Excuse me, could you tell me the way to Oxford Street?
I beg your pardon, do you have the time? *(USA)*

32.2 INTRODUCTIONS

Introducing people

Tony, **this is** Elaine.
Pamela, **meet** Andy./**have you met** Andy?
Mrs Green, **I'd like you to meet/let me introduce you to** Mr Bridges. *(rather formal)*

Saying hello for the first time

Hello, Andy. – **Hello**, Pamela.
Hi, Elaine. – **Hi**, Tony. *(informal)*
How do you do? – **How do you do**? Pleased to meet you. *(rather formal)*
How are you? – **How are you**? *(USA)*

32.3 SAYING HELLO TO SOMEONE YOU KNOW

Saying hello

Hello.
Hi. *(informal)*
Good morning./Good afternoon./Good evening. *(a little more formal than* hello*)*
Morning./Afternoon./Evening. *(Leaving out* good *is less formal.)*

Being polite when saying hello

Nice/Good to see you. **How are you?/How's life?** *(informal)/*
How are things? *(informal)* – **Very well, thank you./Fine, thanks.**
And how are *you***?/And** *you***?** – **OK, thanks./Not too bad, thank you.**

32.4 STARTING A TELEPHONE CONVERSATION

Saying who you are and who you are calling

Hello. **This is** Carl./Carl **here**./Carl **speaking**.
Can I speak to Maria?/**Is** Maria **there**, please?

Asking who the other person is

Is that Mr Tucker? **Is that** Ashford 73780?
Who's that?
Who's speaking?/Who am I speaking to, please? *(more polite)*

32.5 SAYING GOODBYE

Well, I must be going now./I have to go now. **Goodbye,** Phil.
(I'll) see you later./(I'll) be seeing you./See you. **Bye!** *(informal)*
Cheerio!/Cheers!/So long! *(informal)*
Good night. *(at the end of the day)*

32.6 STARTING AND FINISHING A LETTER

Starting a letter

Dear Mrs Moody,/**Dear** Brian,
Dear Sir,/Dear Madam, *(formal)*

Finishing a letter

With best wishes,
Yours sincerely,

Yours faithfully, *(formal)*
Yours,/Love, *(informal)*
Sincerely yours, *(USA)*

32.7 GOOD WISHES

Good wishes for success

All the best. Good luck in your new job.
I hope everything goes all right/goes well for you.
I'd like to wish you every success. *(more formal)*

Good wishes to a third person

Remember me to Chris./**Regards to** Chris./**Love to** Chris.

Good wishes for a holiday etc

Enjoy yourself/yourselves. Have a good time/holiday/trip/journey. **Look after yourself. Take care** on the roads.

Good wishes at special times of the year

Merry Christmas./Happy Christmas. And a **Happy New Year. Have a nice Easter.**
Happy birthday. Many happy returns of the day.

Before drinking

Cheers!/Good health./Here's to you.

There is no special phrase spoken before a meal.

32.8 COMPLIMENTS

Clothes

I like your coat./**That's a lovely** coat./**You look nice in** that coat. – **Thank you.** It's nice of you to say so.

Cooking

That was **a nice/lovely meal.** The steak was **delicious.** – I'm glad you enjoyed it.

32.9 CONGRATULATIONS AND SYMPATHY

Congratulations

I hear you've passed your exam. **Well done!**
Congratulations on passing the exam. – Thank you.

When someone has been unsuccessful

Bad luck./Hard luck. Never mind. Better luck next time.

Sympathy

My father died last week. – Oh, **I'm sorry.**
I was very sorry to hear about your father.

33 Communication: Statements and opinions

33.1 AGREEING WITH OR CORRECTING A STATEMENT

Statement

It's the fifth of May today.
It's the fifth of May today, isn't it?

Agreeing

Yes, it is.
That's right.

Correcting

No, it isn't; it's the sixth.
It's the sixth **actually.**

▷ 8.5 (question tags)

33.2 ASKING ABOUT MEANING

Not understanding

I'm sorry. **I don't understand.**
What do you mean?
I don't get you. *(informal)*
I'm not with you. *(informal)*

Asking the meaning of a word

What's 'cider'? – It's a drink made from apples.
What does 'annually' **mean?** – It means 'every year'.
What's the meaning of the word 'library'? – A library is a place you can borrow books from.

Asking for a word

What do you call it when water becomes ice? – We say it 'freezes'.
What's the word for the thing you put a letter in? – Oh, you mean an 'envelope'.

▷ 34.2 (asking someone to repeat something)

33.3 EXPLANATIONS

Asking for an explanation

Why won't they serve me?
Could you explain why they won't give me a drink?
Could someone **please tell me** what's happening?
I don't understand why we have to go.
I just **don't see** why the pub has to close now.

Giving an explanation

The reason is that it's eleven o'clock.
Well, **the thing is** pubs can only open till eleven.
It's like this, you see. There's a law which says ...

Saying that you understand

I see.
I understand now, thank you.

33.4 BEING SURE AND UNSURE

Being sure

I'm sure/I'm certain/I know there's a bank in this street.
There'**ll** be one here./There **must** be one here. ▷ 7.9
There's **certainly/definitely** one in the next street.

Being less sure

I think/I should think/I believe we have to turn right here.
I don't think/I doubt if we should go left.
I suppose/I expect that's the road to the village.
Maybe/Perhaps we can go straight on. *(not very sure)*
That **may/might/could** be the road to the village. *(not very sure)* ▷ 7.7

Being unsure

I don't know/I'm not sure/I've no idea how far it is to the village.

33.5 OPINIONS

Asking for an opinion

What do you think about the strike?
What's your opinion of the workers' action?
Do you agree with/Are you in favour of the workers getting more money?

Giving an opinion

Well, personally, **I think/I believe/I('d) say/I feel** they should go back to work.
As far as I can see,/As far as I'm concerned,/It seems to me/In my opinion, the workers are badly paid.
I'm convinced the workers are right. *(emphatic)*

Agreeing with an opinion

I (quite) agree./That's right./Quite./Exactly./Of course.

Disagreeing with an opinion

I don't agree/I disagree.
I wouldn't say that./I'm not so sure./I wonder./Do you really think so? *(more polite)*
But **don't you think** … ?/Well, **I think** …/But **on the other hand** …

▷ 36.1 (approving and disapproving)

33.6 PREDICTIONS

Brazil **will** win the World Cup. ▷ 4.1

West Germany have a good team. I think they**'re going to** win. ▷ 4.2

I bet/I expect it'll be exciting.

I guess a South American country will win. *(USA)*

The Italians **are sure to** do well/**are bound to** do well.

I'm sure the Italians are going to do well.

33.7 IMAGINING SITUATIONS

Just **imagine** if there was life on Mars.

What if the people there could build spaceships?

Supposing they visited the earth?

I wonder what I'd say to a person from Mars.

▷ 7.10 *(would)*; 13.2 (the unreal present)

34 Communication: Telling and asking people to do things

34.1 ORDERS

Spoken: Open your mouth, please. **Don't** talk. ▷ 6.1

You **must** sleep now. You **mustn't** talk. ▷ 7.4

You**'re to** drink this. You**'re not to** leave any.

I want you to drink it all. ▷ 14.6

Written: Fasten seat belts. **No** smoking. ▷ 15.1

Visitors **shall** not smoke in the hospital. *(formal)*
Nurses **will** wear uniform at all times. *(formal)*

Sometimes we put an order in the form of a request (▷ 34.2) to make it more polite, e.g. *Could you open your mouth, please?*

▷ 39.3,4 (intonation)

34.2 REQUESTS

Making a request

Would you mind taking me to the station?
Would you like to wash up?
Would you pass the butter, please?
Will you wait a moment, please?
Could you tell me when the next train is?
Can I have some water, please?
Open the window, **would you?/will you?/could you?/can you?**
Passengers **are requested to** remain in their seats. *(formal)*

Asking someone to repeat something

Pardon?/Sorry? Could you repeat that, please? I'm sorry, I didn't catch what you said.

Asking someone to move out of the way

Excuse me. Can I get past?

Agreeing to a request

OK./All right./Yes, of course./Sure.
Certainly. *(more formal)*

Refusing a request

Unfortunately I haven't time.
I have to go now, **actually.**
I'm sorry, but I'm just going out.
I'm afraid I can't just at the moment.

Would you mind + -ing form is a polite request. **Would** and **could** are rather more polite than **will** and **can**.

▷ 11.2 (if-clauses); 39.4 (intonation)

34.3 INTENTIONS

I'm going to visit the USA next year. ▷ 4.2

I've decided to spend a holiday there.

I plan to stay for three weeks.

I intend to see as much as I can.

I might go/**I'm thinking of** going to Los Angeles. *(less sure)* ▷ 7.7

34.4 SUGGESTIONS

Making a suggestion

Shall we go for a swim?
What about/How about playing cards/a game of cards?
Why don't we/**Why not** lie in the sun?
Let's go for a walk, **shall we**?. We **could** go to the park. ▷ 6.2, 7.8

Agreeing with a suggestion

Good idea./OK./Fine./Yes, let's do that./Yes, why not?

Disagreeing with a suggestion

Well, **I was just going to** make some coffee.
I don't feel like cards/don't want to play cards, **actually.**
I'm sorry, it's too hot for me. Let's go to the club **instead.**
That would be nice, but I have to meet someone.

34.5 ADVICE

Asking for advice

What **should** I do/**ought** I **to** do about a job? ▷ 7.6
What **would** you do **in my position?/if you were me?** ▷ 7.10
Could you advise me what to do?
I'd like to ask your advice about a job.

Giving advice

I think you **ought to/should/had better** talk to your parents.
If I were you,/If you ask me, I wouldn't leave school yet.
Well, **I'd advise you to** stay at school.
If you want/ask/take my advice, you won't decide in a hurry.
The best thing for you to do is talk to your head teacher.

34.6 WARNINGS

Look out!/Watch out! *(warning of immediate danger)*
Mind those glasses.
Be careful, or there'll be an accident. ▷ 6.1
If you take all those glasses, you**'ll** drop them. ▷ 11.1
They're heavy, **I'm warning you./I warn you./let me warn you.**

34.7 THREATS

Don't move **or I'll** shoot! **I'll** shoot **if** anyone moves. **If** you do anything stupid, **you'll** be sorry. One move **and** you're dead.

34.8 INSISTING

I **really must** have the money today.
I insist on having it now.
I'm sorry to insist, but I need it today.
I'm afraid I **simply can't** wait any longer.
It's absolutely essential you pay me today.

34.9 PERSUADING

Why don't you join the youth club? – I don't want to.
Why not? All your friends go there. – Yes, but I don't want to.
Oh, **go on./come on.** You could try it. You might enjoy it. – Well, I don't know. I'll think about it.
Look, it would be better than doing nothing, wouldn't it?
You **really must** get out sometimes. – Oh, **all right** then. I'll go next week.

34.10 PROMISES

You'**ll**/You **will**/You **shall** get your money back.
I'**ll**/I **will**/I **shall** give it you back by the weekend.
I **promise** I **won't**/I **shan't** forget.

34.11 OFFERING AND REFUSING

Offering to help

Let me help you. **Can I** carry that suitcase. **I'll** take this bag, shall I? **Shall I** carry it for you? **Would you like me to** get you a taxi?
Allow me. *(formal)*

Offering e.g. food or drink

Would you like/Will you have/Won't you have something to eat?
(Do) have some tea. *(rather more informal)*

Accepting an offer

Yes, please. **Thank you** very much.

Refusing an offer

(of help) **No, thank you.** It's all right. I can manage.
(of food or drink) **No, thank you.**/Not just now, thank you.

Refusing to do something

I won't pay/**I'm not going to** pay/**I refuse to** pay 50p to go in.

34.12 INVITATIONS

Giving an invitation

Would you like to have dinner with us? ▷ 16.2
Will you have/**Won't you** have dinner with us?
(**Do**) come and see us tomorrow. *(rather informal)*
What about coming/**How about** coming to our house? *(rather informal)*
Do you feel like coming/**Do you want to** come to a party? *(rather informal)*

Accepting an invitation

That's very nice of you. **Thank you./Yes, fine.** I'll look forward to it.
Yes, **that'd be nice/lovely.** I'd be delighted to come.

Refusing an invitation

Well, **that's very kind of you, but** I won't be here tomorrow.
I'd love to, but I'm afraid I have some work to do.
Well, **thank you very much, but** I'm afraid I can't.
I'm afraid I won't be here, **but thank you all the same.**

34.13 THANKS

Thanking someone

Thanks./Thanks a lot./Thanks very much. *(informal)*
Thank you./Thank you very much.
That's very good/kind/nice of you. **Thank you very much indeed.** I'm very grateful to you. *(emphatic)*

Answering someone who thanks you

That's all right/OK.
It's a pleasure./Not at all./Don't mention it.
You're welcome. *(mostly USA)*

There is often no answer after thank you etc in British English.

35 Communication: Feelings

35.1 BEING PLEASED AND ANNOYED

Being pleased

I've won £100. –
That's **good/great.**
That's **wonderful/marvellous/terrific.** *(more emphatic)*

Being annoyed

The train is half an hour late. –
Oh, no!/Oh, dear. What a nuisance!
Oh, hell!/Damn! *(swear words)*

35.2 LIKES AND DISLIKES

Likes

This place is **nice/great/lovely**, isn't it?
I like/I love/I enjoy/I'm fond of the seaside.
It's my **favourite** kind of holiday. There's nothing I like better.

Dislikes

This programme's **not very good/not very interesting.**
It's **terrible/awful.** *(more emphatic)*
I don't like/I dislike/I hate watching quiz programmes.
I can't bear/I can't stand quiz programmes. *(more emphatic)*
I can't bear to watch them.

▷ 16.2 (the infinitive and the -ing form)

35.3 WISHING AND HOPING

Wishing

I wish the weather was nicer. ▷ 13.3
If only the sun would shine. **Why can't** these clouds go away?
I'd like to/I'd love to/I want to lie in the sun. **I want** my back **to** get brown. ▷ 14.6; 16.2
I'm dying to sit on the beach. **I'm dying for** a drink. *(more emphatic)*

Hoping

I hope it's nice later. **Let's hope** we can go on the beach.

35.4 PREFERENCES

Asking about preferences

Would you prefer/Do you prefer tea or coffee?
Would you rather have milk or cream?

Expressing preference

I'd prefer to go out **rather than** sit here.
I usually **prefer** walking **to** doing nothing./**like** walking **better than** doing nothing.
I'd rather do something **than** just sit. **I'd rather not** stay here.

Having no preference

I don't mind/I don't care what we do. It's all the same to me.
It doesn't matter to me where we go.

35.5 SHOWING SURPRISE AND INTEREST

Surprise

I'm going to give up my job. –
You're not, are you? ▷ 8.5
Are you **really**? ▷ 9.1
Really? Well, **that is a surprise.**
Good heavens./Good Lord. I don't believe it.

You aren't going to give up your job, are you? ▷ 8.5
Are you **really** going to give up your job? Aren't you going to go on working? ▷ 8.3

Interest

I'm going to give up my job. –
You are, are you? ▷ 8.5
Oh, are you? ▷ 9.1
Oh, **really? That *is* interesting.**

So you're going to give up your job, are you? ▷ 8.5

35.6 REGRET

Unfortunately/I'm afraid the car won't start.
What a pity/shame we're going to be late.
It's a pity/shame we're going to be late.
I'm sorry to say/**I regret** to say we're going to miss the show.
I'm sorry not to have seen/**I regret** not having seen the show.

▷ 36.4 (apologies)

35.7 WORRY

Asking someone what the matter is

What's the matter?/What's wrong?/What's up?
(Is) anything wrong/the matter?

Being worried

I'm worried about the money.

Telling someone not to worry

Don't worry./There's nothing to worry about.
It's all right./It's OK./It doesn't matter.

36 Communication: Right and wrong

36.1 APPROVING AND DISAPPROVING

Approving

I'm glad/I'm pleased the government are increasing the tax on petrol.
The government are **right**/It's **right** to do it.
They're **doing the right thing. It's a good idea.**
I approve of them making petrol more expensive. **I'm in favour** of it.
I'm all for it. *(informal)*

Disapproving

People **oughtn't to** drive/**shouldn't** drive big cars. ▷ 7.6
It's **wrong/not right** to use so much petrol.
I **don't approve** of/I **disapprove** of people using up so much energy. **I'm against** people driving big cars.

▷ 33.5 (opinions)

36.2 BLAMING SOMEONE

The accident was the lorry driver**'s fault.**
I blame the lorry driver. The lorry driver was **to blame.**
He **ought to have/should have** stopped. ▷ 7.6, 15

36.3 COMPLAINING

I'm afraid I have a complaint to make about the food.
I'm sorry to have to say this, but the service isn't very good.
Look, **I really must protest** about the condition of my room.
Can't something be done to stop the noise?

36.4 APOLOGIES

Making an apology

I'm sorry I've damaged your car.
I'm very/extremely/awfully/terribly sorry.
I apologize/I do apologize. ▷ 28.6
Please accept my apologies. *(formal)*
Excuse me./Pardon me. *(starting or interrupting a conversation; after sneezing, coughing etc)*

Accepting an apology

That's all right/OK, as long as you pay for the damage.
It doesn't matter.
Forget it. *(informal)*

37 Punctuation

37.1 THE SENTENCE

1 **W**e'll go for a walk now**.** **B**ut bring your coat**.**
2 **D**o you want to go to **H**yde **P**ark**?** – **S**hall we look at the shops first**?** – **A**re they open on **S**aturdays**?**
3 **L**ook what **I**'ve got**!** – **W**hat a fantastic hat**!**

At the end of a sentence we put
1 a full stop (**.**) after a statement or imperative.
2 a question mark (**?**) after a question.
3 an exclamation mark (**!**) after an exclamation.

We write a capital letter (a big letter)
1 at the beginning of a sentence (e.g. *We* ... or *But* ...).
2 at the beginning of each word in a name (e.g. *Hyde Park*) and at the beginning of days and months (e.g. *Saturday*),
but not in other nouns (e.g. *shops*).
3 for the word *I*.

37.2 THE SEMI-COLON

The farmer and his sons start work at six o'clock every morning; they have to get up early because there is always so much to do.

We use a semi-colon (**;**) between two main clauses when the second main clause does not begin with a conjunction.

37.3 THE COMMA

We use a comma to show a pause in a sentence. A comma means a shorter pause than a semi-colon (**;**) or a full stop (**.**) .
We cannot always say that we **must** or **must not** put a comma in an English sentence. The writer can often choose whether to put a comma or not.

Main clauses

1 The police are looking for Mr Sims, but they can't find him.
2 The police are looking for Mr Sims but can't find him.

1 We usually put a comma between two main clauses when the second clause begins with **but, and** or **or**.
2 We do not usually put a comma when we leave out the subject of the second main clause (e.g. *they*).

Other clauses

1a When they arrived at the house, the two men waited in the car for a moment.
b The two men waited in the car for a moment when they arrived at the house.
2a Mr Sims is in trouble with the police, David said.
b David said that Mr Sims was in trouble with the police.
3a Mr Sims, who lives in that house, is in trouble with the police.
b The man who lives in that house is in trouble with the police.

We put a comma
1a usually after a sub clause (e.g. a clause with *when, if* or *because*) when it comes before the main clause.
2a after a reported clause when it comes before the main clause. ▷ 37.5
3a before and after a non-defining relative clause. ▷ 22.12

But:
1b not usually when the sub clause is after the main clause.
2b not before a reported clause or before other clauses with **that**.
3b not with a defining relative clause. ▷ 22.12

The infinitive

The police came to the house to ask him some questions.

We do not use a comma before an infinitive.

Adverb phrases

1 On Thursday afternoon, the police broke into the house.
2 The police broke into the house on Thursday afternoon.

1 We sometimes put a comma after an adverb phrase at the beginning of a sentence.
2 We do not usually put a comma before an adverb phrase at the end of a sentence.

Phrases adding extra information

Mr Sim, the owner of the house, was not there.

We put a comma before and after a phrase which adds extra information about something.

Linking words and adverbs

1 Mr Sims, however, was not there.
2a However, Mr Sims was not there.
b Mr Sims was not there, however.
3a Of course, Mr Sims was not there.
b Mr Sims was not there, of course.
4a Can you help us, please?
b No, I can't.

1 We usually put a comma before and after a linking word in the middle of a sentence, e.g. **however, on the other hand, as a result, for example.**
2 We usually put a comma after or before the same linking words at the beginning or end of a sentence.
3 We sometimes put a comma after or before an adverb referring to a whole sentence. ▷ 24.13
4 We usually put a comma before **please** and after **yes** or **no**.

Addressing a person by name

Have you seen your neighbour today, Mrs Golding?
Dear Mr Bright,
Thank you for your letter... ▷ 32.6

We put a comma before or after the name of the person we are speaking or writing to.

Lists

Inside the room there was a table, two chairs, a lamp and a television set.

We put commas in a list of more than two things.

37.4 THE APOSTROPHE

1 Is that your brother**'s** bicycle outside the Johnson**s'**?
2 No, it isn**'**t. He**'**s got a blue bicycle.

We use the apostrophe
1 in the possessive form of nouns ▷ 18.4
2 in short forms ▷ 38.2

37.5 QUOTATION MARKS

David said, **'**Mr Sims is in trouble with the police.**'**
'Mr Sims is in trouble with the police,**'** David said./said David.

We use quotation marks ('...') before and after direct speech.
We usually put a comma before or after the direct speech.

▷ 37.3 (reported speech – see under *Other clauses*)

37.6 THE HYPHEN

1a That's a **police dog**.
b I've rung the **police-station**.
c Here's a **policeman**.
2a I've got a **motor cycle**.
b I've got a **motor-cycle**.
c I've got a **motorcycle**.
3a Don't **overfill** the tank.
b Don't **over-fill** the tank.
4a There's a **three-mile-long** tunnel.
b This is a **steel-producing** town.
5a We can **re-use** these bottles.
b The player has **re-signed** for the club.
c The player has **resigned** from the club.

1a We write some compound nouns as two words.
b We write some compound nouns with a hyphen.
c We write some compound nouns as one word.

▷ 29.2 (compound nouns)

2 Some compound nouns can be two words (a), with a hyphen (b) or one word (c), so with many nouns we cannot say that we **must** or **must not** put a hyphen.
3 We sometimes use a hyphen in compounds with **over** and **under**. ▷ 29.9
4 We use a hyphen in compound adjectives. ▷ 29.7, 8
5 We use a hyphen after **re** (= again)
a before a vowel, e.g. **re-use, re-enter, re-open**.
b, c to make a difference between two verbs, e.g. **re-sign** [riːˈsaɪn] (= sign again) and **resign** [riˈsain] (= give up a job). ▷ 29.10 (*re-*)

38 Weak forms and short forms

38.1 WEAK FORMS

If your ′dog ′wants his ′dinner, I've ′got some ′meat and ′biscuits for him.
[jə] [ɪz] [v] [səm] [n] [fər ɪm]

We put stress (′) on nouns, verbs, adjectives and adverbs. ▷ 39.1
A lot of words which are not stressed have a weak (unstressed) form, e.g. *your* is [jə], not [jɔː], *his* is [ɪz], not [hɪz].
Some unstressed words do **not** have a weak form, e.g. *if* [ɪf], *I* [aɪ].
Some words which have a weak form also have a written short form, e.g. *'ve* (have). ▷ 38.2

38.2 SHORT FORMS

1a	Nora:	We'**ve** had nice weather here.
b	Sammy:	My back'**s** brown already.
c	Nora:	What'**s** it going to be like today?
d	Joe:	There'**ll** be more sunshine.
e	Nora:	That'**s** good.
f	Sammy:	It has**n't** rained at all yet.
2		Dear Bill, We'**ve** had nice weather here. My back'**s** brown already...

Form When we use a short form, we leave out part of the word we are writing. We put an apostrophe (') instead of the missing part.

Short forms

'm	= am	**'ve**	= have	**won't**	= will not
're	= are	**'d**	= had *or* would	**n't**	= not
's	= is *or* has	**'ll**	= will *or* shall		

NOTE **it isn't** = it is not **they won't** = they will not
it's not = it is not **they'll not** = they will not

Use We can use a short form only if the word is unstressed. ▷ 38.1; 39.1

We can use short forms
a after a pronoun
b sometimes after a noun
c sometimes after a question word
d after **there**
e for **is** after **that** and **here**
f for **not** after an auxiliary or modal verb

We use short forms
1 when we write down an informal conversation.
2 in informal writing, e.g. in a postcard to a friend.

39 Stress and intonation

39.1 STRESS

The ′first ′train is at ′half past ′seven.
I'll ′drive you to the ′station to′morrow.

We put stress (′) on words that are important for the meaning of the sentence.
Stressed words are spoken more loudly than unstressed words. ▷ 38.1 (weak forms)
Most stressed words are nouns (e.g. *train*), verbs (e.g. *drive*), adjectives (e.g. *first*) or adverbs (e.g. *tomorrow*).

39.2 INTONATION

The first train is at half past ↘ **sev**en.
The first train is at half past ↗ **sev**en?

The speaker's voice falls (↘) or rises (↗) at the end of a sentence. A fall or rise on a word makes it more important than the other stressed words.
A rise has a different meaning from a fall. A change in intonation can change a statement into a question.

39.3 FALLING INTONATION

1 These ↘ **coats** are nice.
2 Give me the ↘ **blue** one.
3 Which do you like ↘ **best**?

We use a falling intonation in
1 statements, when we are sure about what we say.
2 orders.
3 w-questions.
But ▷ 39.4

39.4 RISING INTONATION

1 Did you have a good ↗ **hol**iday?
2 You had a good ↗ **hol**iday?
3 Where did you ↗ **go**?
4 Can we see your ↗ **pho**tos?
5 I can show you them ↗ **now**.

We use a rising intonation in
1 yes/no questions.
2 questions in statement form.
3 w-questions which show a polite interest.
4 polite orders and requests.
5 statements, when we are not sure about what we say, or when the statement needs an answer.

40 List of common irregular verbs

Verb**	Past tense	Past participle
awake	awoke	awaked/awoke
be (am, is, are)	was, were	been
beat	beat	beaten
become	became	become
begin	began	begun
bend	bent	bent
bet	bet/betted	bet
bite	bit	bitten/bit
blow	blew	blown
break	broke	broken
bring	brought	brought
build	built	built
burn	burnt/burned*	burnt/burned
burst	burst	burst
buy	bought	bought
catch	caught	caught
choose	chose	chosen
come	came	come
cost	cost	cost
cut	cut	cut
deal	dealt [e]	dealt [e]
dig	dug	dug
do (does [ʌ])	did	done
draw	drew	drawn
dream	dreamed [i:]/ dreamt [e]	dreamed [i:]/ dreamt [e]
drink	drank	drunk
drive	drove	driven
eat	ate [et]/[eɪt] (*USA*)	eaten
fall	fell	fallen
feed	fed	fed
feel	felt	felt
fight	fought	fought
find	found	found
flee	fled	fled
fly	flew	flown
forbid	forbade [æ]/forbad	forbidden
forget	forgot	forgotten
forgive	forgave	forgiven
freeze	froze	frozen
get	got	got/gotten (*USA*)
give	gave	given
go (goes)	went	gone ▷ 5.4
grow	grew	grown
hang	hung	hung
have (has)	had	had
hear	heard [ɜ:]	heard [ɜ:]
hide	hid	hidden
hit	hit	hit
hold	held	held
hurt	hurt	hurt
keep	kept	kept
know	knew	known
lay	laid	laid
lead	led	led
learn	learnt/learned*	learnt/learned
leave	left	left
lend	lent	lent
let	let	let
lie	lay	lain
light	lighted/lit	lighted/lit
lose	lost	lost
make	made	made
mean	meant [e]	meant [e]
meet	met	met
pay	paid	paid
put	put	put
read	read [e]	read [e]
ride	rode	ridden
ring	rang	rung
rise	rose	risen
run	ran	run
say (says [e])	said [e]	said [e]
see	saw	seen
seek	sought	sought
sell	sold	sold
send	sent	sent
set	set	set
shake	shook	shaken
shine	shone [ɒ]	shone [ɒ]
shoot	shot	shot
show	showed	shown/showed
shut	shut	shut
sing	sang	sung
sink	sank	sunk
sit	sat	sat
sleep	slept	slept
smell	smelt/smelled*	smelt/smelled
speak	spoke	spoken
spell	spelt/spelled*	spelt/spelled
spend	spent	spent
spoil	spoilt/spoiled*	spoilt/spoiled
spread	spread	spread
spring	sprang	sprung
stand	stood	stood
steal	stole	stolen
stick	stuck	stuck
sting	stung	stung
stink	stank/stunk	stunk
strike	struck	struck
sweep	swept	swept
swim	swam	swum
swing	swung	swung
take	took	taken
teach	taught	taught
tear	tore	torn
tell	told	told
think	thought	thought
throw	threw	thrown
understand	understood	understood
wake	woke/waked	woken/waked
wear	wore	worn
win	won	won
write	wrote	written

* **NOTE** Some verbs have two past forms, e.g. *learnt/learned*. The form with **-t** is more usual in British English and the form with **-ed** in American English. **Burned**, **learned**, **smelled**, **spelled** and **spoiled** can be pronounced with [t] or [d].

**and irregular simple present forms

Index

a/an 19
ability 7.2
a bit 20.18,19; 24.12
able to 7.2,16
about to 4.8
above 25.1
accepting 34.11,12
across 25.1
additions to statements 9.1
adjective + preposition + -ing form 15.4
adjectives 23; compound 29.7,8; -ing/-ed form 17.1; after *look, smell,* etc. 24.6; after *something* etc. 20.14; + *one/ones* 20.11; + infinitive 14.2; possessive 20.5; demonstrative 20.10
adverb phrases, position 1.5; place and time 24.10; punctuation 37.3
adverbs 24; spelling 30.3,6; punctuation 37.3
advice 34.5; reporting 12.7
advice 18.11
a few 20.15,18,19
after preposition 25.4; conjunction 15.2; 17.3; 27.2
ago 25.7
agree 10.9; 12.1; 15.4; 16.1
agreeing 33.1,5; 34.4
agreement of subject and verb 18.12–15
a little 20.15,18,19; 24.12
all 20.19,20
allow 14.8,10
allowed to 7.3,16; 14.10
almost 24.12
along 25.1
a lot 20.15,18,19
alphabet 31.13
also 27.3
alternative questions 8.2
alternatives 27.4
although 15.2; 17.5; 27.6
always 2.7; 24.11
am 2.1,3
an 19.1
and 27.1,3; with comparatives 23.6
being annoyed 35.1
another 20.17
answering questions 8.4
-ant 29.1
any 20.12,13,18,19
anyone, -thing etc 20.14
apologies 36.4
apostrophe 18.4–6; 30.6; 37.4
appear 20.2; 24.6
approving 36.1
are 2.1,3
arrangements 4.4,7
articles 19
as comparison 23.4; time 27.2; reason 27.7
as a result 27.9
as ... as 23.4
as if 13.2
ask 12.1,6; 14.5
asking about meaning 33.2
as long as 27.11
as soon as 27.2
as well 27.3
at place 25.1,2; time 25.3
auxiliary verbs 5; 28.6
away from 25.1

be present 2.1; past 3.1; uses 5.2–4; auxiliary 5.8
be able to 7.2,16
be about to 4.8
be allowed to 7.3,16; 14.10
because 1.6; 17.4; 27.1,7
because of 27.7
been in perfect tenses 3.4,8,10; in the passive 10.3
been to 5.4
before preposition 25.4; conjunction 15.2; 27.12
begin 16.2
be going to 4.2,3; past plans 4.10
behind 25.1
being 10.4; 15.6
beliefs 19.8; 29.5
believe 2.5; 9.2; 10.9,10; 15.4
below 25.1
best adjective 23.3; adverb 24.8
be to arrangements 4.7; orders 12.6
better: see *best*
between 25.1
be used to 15.4
bit + *of* 18.11; see also *a bit*
blaming 36.2
-body 20.14
both 20.20; ... *and* 27.3
but 27.1,6
by time 25.5; place 25.1; means 25.8,9; agent 10.2;

can 7.2,3,9
capital letters 37.1
cardinal numbers 31.1
certainty 7.9
clauses 1.6; 27.1
collective nouns 18.14
comma 27.1; 37.3
commands: see orders
communication 32–36
comparatives: see comparison
comparison, adjectives 23.2,3,4–8; adverbs 24.7,8; spelling 30.3,5,6
complaining 36.3
compliments 32.8
compounds, nouns 29.2,3; adjectives 29.7,8; *someone* etc 20.14; with *-ever* 27.12; hyphen 37.6
concord 18.12–15
conditional clauses 11; 27.11
congratulations 32.9
conjunctions 27; + -ing form 15.2; 17.2; + -ed form 17.5
connecting words 27; punctuation 37.3
consequently 27.9
contact clauses, relative 22.4,5; reported 12.1
continue 16.2
continuous infinitive 14.14
continuous tenses, present 2.3; past 3.7; present perfect 3.8; past perfect 3.10; future 4.6; with modals 7.14; passive 10.4
contracted forms: see short forms
contrast 27.5,6
correcting 33.1
could 7.2,8
countable and uncountable nouns 18.8–11; 20.3,15–20

daily 24.4
dare 7.13
dates 31.11
deciding 4.1–3
decimals 31.5
defining relative clauses 22.1,12; 27.1
definite article: see *the*
degree adverbs 24.12

demonstrative adjectives 20.10,11,20
demonstrative pronouns 20.10
did uses 5.7,8; in simple past 3.3; with *have* 3.2; with *used to* 3.11
direct object 1.4; 18.3; passive 10.1,6; phrasal verbs 26.2; emphasis 28.2
dis- 29.6
disagreeing 33.1,5; 34.4
disapproving 36.1
dislikes 35.2
do uses 5.7; auxiliary 5.8; in simple present 2.4; with *have* 5.6; imperative 6.1; with *let's* 6.2; emphatic 28.6
doubling of consonants 30.5
down 25.1
during 25.4

each 20.11,13,20
each other 20.9
early 24.4
-ed form, in perfect tenses 3.4,6; with modals 7.15; in the passive 10; as adjective 17.1; 29.7; reason 17.4; after conjunctions 17.5; in relative clauses 22.11; spelling 30.3,5,6; pronunciation 30.4; irregular forms 40; see also *been*
e.g. 27.13
either 9.1; 27.4
elder, eldest 23.8
emphasis 28
emphatic pronouns 20.8; 28.5.
endings, pronunciation and spelling 30
enjoy 16.1; 20.7
enough 24.12
-ent 29.1
-er 29.1
-ess 29.1
even 24.15
even if 27.11
even though 27.6
ever 3.4; 24.11
-ever 27.12
every 20.11,13
everyone, -thing etc 20.14
exclamations *what a* 19.9; punctuation 37.1
explanations 33.3
fairly 24.12
falling intonation 39.3
far 23.3; 24.8
farther, farthest 23.3,8; 24.8
feelings 2.4; 35
a few 20.15,18,19
fewer, fewest 20.16
first, second etc. 31.2; + infinitive 22.10
for time 3.4,8; 25.7; + indirect object 18.3; + -ing form 15.2; 27.8; + noun phase + infinitive 14.11
force 14.8
for example 27.13
forget 16.2
fractions 31.4
frequency adverbs 24.11
from place 25.1; time 25.6
full stop 37.1
further, furthest 23.3,8; 24.8
future 4
future continuous tense 4.6
future perfect tense 4.9

gerund: see -ing form
get in the passive 10.7
get something done 10.8
going to 4.2,3; past plans 4.10
gone to 5.4
good comparison 23.3
goodbye 32.5
good wishes 32.7
got see *have got*
greetings 32.3,5

habits 2.4; 7.11
had possession 3.2; in perfect tenses 3.6,10; past participle 3.4
had better 34.5
half 19.10; 20.19; 31.4
happen 20.2
hard, hardly 24.4,5
has: see *have*
hate 16.2
have uses 5.5,8; possession 2.2; 3.2; in perfect tenses 3.4,6,8,10; with modals 7.15; in American English 5.6
have got present 2.2; past 3.2
have (got) to 7.4,16
have something done 10.8
having (been) + -ed form 17.3,4
he 20.1
hear: see *see*
hello 32.3
help + infinitive 14.9; *can't help* 16.1
helping verbs 5; 28.6
her 20.1; possessive 20.5
here emphatic use 28.7
hers 20.5
herself 20.7,8; 28.5
high, highly 24.4,5
him 20.1
himself 20.7,8; 28.5
his 20.5
hoping 35.3
how means 21.1; 25.8,9; in question phrases 21.4
however contrast 27.6; 37.3; compound 27.12
how long 3.4,8
how many/much 20.18,19; 21.4
hyphen 37.6

I 20.1
if = *whether* 12.5,6
if-clauses 11; 27.11; order of clauses 1.6; 27.1; with -ed form 17.5
il- 29.6
im- 29.6
imagining 7.10; 33.7
imperative 6.1
in 25.1–3
in- 29.6
indefinite article 19
indefinite pronouns 20.14
indirect object 1.4; 18.3; in the passive 10.6
indirect speech 12; 27.1; passive 10.10
infinitive 14; and -ing form 16; in relative clauses 22.10; purpose 27.8; punctuation 37.3
information 18.11
in front of 25.1
-ing form 15; 29.4; and infinitive 16; as adjective 17.1; 29.7 time 17.2,3; reason 17.4; in continuous tenses 2.3; 3.7,8,10; 4.6; 10.4; with modals 7.14; in relative clauses 22.11; spelling 30.3,5,6
in order to 27.8
inside 25.1
insisting 34.8; reporting 12.7

in spite of 27.6; + -ing form 15.2
instead of 15.2
intend 16.2
intentions 4.2; 34.3
interrogative adjectives/ pronouns/adverbs 21; + infinitive 14.12
interrogatives: see questions
into 25.1
intonation 39.2–4; emphasis 28.1; question tags 8.5
introductions 32.2
invitations 34.12; imperative 6.1; reporting 12.7
ir- 29.6
irregular comparison, adjectives 23.3; adverbs 24.8
irregular plurals 18.2
irregular verbs 40
is 2.1,3
-ism 29.5
-ist 29.1,5
it 20.1–3; and *there* 5.3; + passive 10.9; for emphasis 28.3
its 20.5
itself 20.7,8; 28.5

jobs 29.1; with *a/an* 19.8
just time 3.4; degreee 24.12

kind of 21.4
know 2.5; 10.10; 12.1

last 23.8
late, lately 24.4,5
latest 23.8
least 20.16; 23.5
leaving out words 9.1,3,4
less 20.16; 23.5
let 14.8,10
let's 6.2
letters 32.6; 37.3
like verb 2.4,5; 16.2; preposition 21.5; 27.13
likes 35.2
linking words 27; 37.3
a little 20.15,18,19; 24.12
a long way 23.3; 24.8
a lot 20.15,18,19
love 2.5; 16.2
-ly 24.2; 30.3,6
main clauses and sub clauses 13; 27.1; see also sub clauses
make 14.8,10
-man 29.1
manner adverbs 24.3
many 20.15,18,19
may 7.3,7
me 20.1
means 25.8,9
measurements 31.12; + singular verb 18.15
might 7.7
mind 7.3; 16.1; 34.2
mine 20.5
mis- 29.11
modal verbs 7; *will* and *shall* 4.11; + passive 10.5; in if-clauses 11; in reported speech 12.3
money 31.9
more 20.16,17; in comparatives 23.2,6,7
most 20.16,19,20; 24.5; in superlatives 23.2
mostly 24.5
much 20.15,18,19; 24.12
must 7.4,9
mustn't 7.4,5; 12.6
my 20.5
myself 20.7,8; 28.5

nationality 23.10; with *a/an* 19.8
near 25.1; and *nearly* 24.4,5
nearest, next 23.8
nearly 24.5
necessity 7.4,5
needn't 7.4,5,15
negative questions 8.3
negatives 1.2; 8.1; 9.2
neither 9.1; 27.4
never 3.4,11; 24.11
news 18.11,13
next, nearest 23.8
next to 25.1
no 20.12,18,19
non-defining relative clauses 22.1,12; 27.1
none 20.18,19
no one, nothing etc 20.14
nor 9.1; 27.4
not: see negatives
not only ... (but) also 27.3
nouns 18; word-building 26.6; 29.1–5; as adjectives 23.11; + infinitive 14.3
numbers 31; + *of* 20.19; in compound adjectives 29.8

object: see direct object, indirect object
object pronouns 18.3; 20.1
obligation 7.6
of possessive 18.7; 20.6; quantity 18.9; 20.19; 27.4; + *which* 22.8
off 25.1
offers 34.11; imperative 6.1; reporting 12.7
often 24.11
on place 25.1; time 25.3; + -ing form 15.2; 17.2
once, twice etc 31.3
one 20.3,4,11; 31.1
-one 20.14
ones 20.11
only 24.15; + infinitive 22.10
on the other hand 27.5
onto 25.1
opinions 33.5
opposite 25.1
opposites 29.6
or 27.1,4
-or 29.1
order of words: see word order
orders 6.1; 34.1; with if-clauses 11.2; reporting 12.6
ordinal numbers 31.2; + infinitive 22.10
ought to 7.6
our, ours 20.5

ourselves 20.7,8; 28.5
out of 25.1
outside 25.1
over 25.1
over- 29.9; 37.6

pair nouns 18.12
participle: see -ing form, -ed form
passive 10; 20.4; + infinitive 14.10; phrasal verbs and prepositional verbs 26.4; reported orders 12.6
passive infinitive 14.14
passive -ing form 15.6
past 25.1; 31.10
past continuous 3.7; passive 10.4
past participle: see -ed form
past perfect 3.6; passive 10.3; in if-clauses 11.1; in reported speech 12.3
past perfect continuous 3.10
past plans 4.10

past tenses 3; 13; in reported speech 12.3,4
people 20.4
percentages 31.6
perception: see verbs of perception
perfect infinitive 14.14
perfect -ing form 17.3
perfect tenses, present 3.4; past 3.6; passive 10.3
permission 7.3
-person 29.1
personal pronouns 20.1–4; after *than* 23.2
persuading 34.9
phrasal-prepositional verbs 26.5
phrasal verbs 26
piece 18.11
place, prepositions 25.1,2; adverbs 24.10; possessive form 18.5
place names 19.5
being pleased 35.1
plural of nouns 18.1,2; 30.2,6; pronunciation 30.1
police 18.14
position of adverbs 24.9; emphasis 28.2
possession *have (got)* 2.2; 3.2; see also possessive
possessive adjectives 20.5; after *all, both* 20.20; + -ing form 15.5
possessive form of nouns 18.4–6; + -ing form 15.5; pronunciation 30.1; apostrophe 30.6; 37.4
possessive pronouns 20.5,6
possibility 7.8; 11
predictions 4.1,2; 33.6
prefer 16.2
preferences 35.4
prefixes 29.6,9–11
prepositional verbs 26.3,4
prepositions 25; + -ing form 15.2,4; + indirect object 18.3; in questions 21.5; in relative clauses 22.5,7; after verbs 26.3; after nouns 29.4; see also *at, by, of* etc
present continuous 2.3,5–7; future meaning 4.4; passive 10.4
present participle: see -ing form
present perfect 3.4,5,9; passive 10.3
present perfect continuous 3.8,9
present tenses 2
price 19.11; 31.9
probability 7.7; 11
progressive tenses: see continuous tenses
promises 34.10; reporting 12.7
pronouns 20; relative 22; + infinitive 14.3; two objects 18.3; after *than* 23.2
pronunciation, endings 30.1,4; weak forms 38.1; *the* 19.1; see also intonation, stress
provided (that) 27.11
punctuation 37
purpose 27.8

quantifiers 20
quantity 18.9; 20
questions 1.3; 8.2; negative 8.3; answering 8.4; reporting 12.5 with prepositions 21.5; punctuation 37.1
question tags 8.5
question words 21; + infinitive 14.12
quite 24.12; + *a/an* 19.10
quotation marks 37.5

rather 24.12; with *a/an* 19.10
re- 29.10
reason 27.7; -ing/-ed form 17.4
reflexive pronouns 20.7
refusing 34.11,12; reporting 12.7
regret 35.6
relative clauses 22; 27.1; for emphasis 28.3
relative pronouns 22
remember 16.2
replacing words 9.1,2
reported speech 12; 27.1; passive 10.10
reporting verbs 12.1
requests 34.2; with if-clauses 11.2; reporting 12.6
result 27.9,10
rising intonation 39.4
round 25.1

's 18.4; 37.4
say reporting 12.1,2; passive 10.9,10
see with *can* 2.5; 7.2; + infinitive/-ing form 16.3; passive 10.11
seem 2.5; 16.1; 20.2; 24.6
-self/-selves 20.7,8; 28.5
semi-colon 37.2
sequence of tenses 13.1
shall 4.11
she 20.1
short forms 38.2
should 7.6,12
simple past 3.3,5; passive 10.1; in if-clauses 11; in reported speech 12.3,4; spelling 30.3, 5,6; pronunciation 30.4; irregular forms 40
simple present 2.4–6,8; future meaning 4.5; passive 10.1; in if-clauses 11; spelling 30.2,6; pronunciation 30.1
since preposition 3.4,8; 25.7; clause of time 27.2; clause of reason 27.7; + -ing form 15.2
so degree 24.12; result 27.9, 10; replacing words 9.1,2
so … as 23.4
so as to 27.8
some 19.3; 20.3,12,18,19
some more 20.17
someone, -thing etc 20.14
sometimes 24.11
so that 27.8
so … (that) 27.10.
speed 19.11
spelling, endings 30; capital letters 37.1
start 16.2
starting a conversation 32.1, 3,4
still 24.14
stop 16.2
stress 39.1; emphasis 28.1,6; weak forms 38.1; verb + adverb/preposition 26.4; compound nouns 29.2,3
sub clauses, tenses 4.1; 13; order of clauses 1.6; 27.1; punctuation 37.3
subject 1; of -ing form 15.5
such 19.10; 27.10
such as 27.13
such … (that) 27.10
suffixes 29.1,4,5; *-self/-selves* 20.7; *-one, -thing* etc 20.14; *-ever* 27.12

suggestions 34.4; *let's* 6.2; negative questions 8.3; reporting 12.7
sums 31.7
superlative, adjectives 23.2,3, 5,8; adverbs 24.7,8; + infinitive 22.10; spelling 30.3,5,6
suppose 2.5; 9.2; 10.10; 13.2
being sure and unsure 33.4
surprise 35.5; negative questions 8.3
sympathy 32.9

tags 8.5
telephone numbers 31.8
telephoning 32.4
tell 12.1,6
temperature 31.12
tenses 2-4; 12.2–4; 13
than 23.2
thanking 34.13
that demonstrative 20.10; relative 22.1,3,4,12; in reported speech 12.1; after *so/such* 27.10
the 19; + *one/ones* 20.11; + adjective 23.9; with comparatives 23.7
their, theirs 20.5
them 20.1,3
themselves 20.7–9; 28.5
there and *it* 5.3; emphatic use 28.7
therefore 27.9
these 20.10,11
they 20.1,4
thing 23.9
-thing 20.14
think 2.4,5; 9.2; + *of* 15.4; passive 10.9,10
this 20.10,11
those 20.10,11
thoughts 2.4
threats 34.7; reporting 12.7
through 25.1
till: see *until*
time, prepositions 25.3–7; adverbs 24.10; phrases without *the* 19.6; clauses 27.2; -ing form 17.2,3; possessive form 18.6
time of day 31.10
-tion 29.4
to place 25.1; time 25.6; 31.10; + indirect object 1.4; 18.3; infinitive 14.1
too degree 24.12; = *also* 27.3
towards 25.1
try 16.2

un- 29.6
uncountable nouns 18.8–11; 20.3,15–19
under 25.1
under- 29.9
unless 27.11; + -ed form 17.5
unreal present and past 13.2
until preposition 4.9; 25.5,6; conjunction 27.2; + -ed form 17.5
up 25.1
us 20.1
used to 3.11; 15.4
usually 24.11

verb + adverb 26.1,2,4
verb + infinitive 14.4,7; 16.1,2
verb + -ing form 15.3; 16.1,2
verb-noun 15.1
verb + object + infinitive 14.5, 7,8
verb + preposition 26.3,4
verb + preposition + -ing form 15.4
verbs made into nouns 26.6; 29.4
verbs of perception, with *can* 2.5; 7.2; + infinitive/-ing form 16.3; passive 10.11
verb tenses 2–4; 12.2–4; 13
very 24.12

want 2.4,5; + infinitive 14.6,7
warnings 34.6; imperative 6.1; reporting 12.7
was 3.1,7
was going to 4.10
we 20.1
weak forms 38.1
weight 31.12
well 24.8
were 3.1,7
what question word 21.1–3; in question phrases 21.4; relative pronoun 22.9; for emphasis 28.4; exclamations 19.9
whatever 27.12
what for 21.5
when question word 21.1; conjunction 1.6; 27.1,2; + -ing form 17.5; in relative clauses 22.13
whenever 27.12
where question word 21.1; in relative clauses 22.13
-where 20.14
whereas 27.5
wherever 27.12
whether conditional 27.11; reported questions 12.5; + infinitive 14.12
which question word 21.3; + *one/ones* 20.11; relative pronoun 22
whichever 27.12
while time 27.2; + -ing form 15.2; contrast 27.5
who question word 21.1–3; relative pronoun 22
whoever 27.12
whole 20.20
whom 22.6,7,12
whose question word 21.1; relative pronoun 22.8, 12
why question word 21.1; 27.7,8; in relative clauses 22.13
will 4.1,3; 7.9,11; uses 4.11; passive 10.5; in if-clauses 11; in reported speech 12.3
wish 13.3
wishing 13.3; 35.3
with 25.9
without 15.2
-woman 29.1
won't: see *will*
word-building 29
word order 1; clauses and conjunctions 27; adverbs 24.9; *all, most* etc 20.20; passive 10.1; phrasal verbs 26.2–4; emphasis 28.2,7
worry 35.7
worse, worst adjective 23.3; adverb 24.8
would 7.10–12; in if-clauses 11
would like 14.6; 16.2
would rather 13.2; 35.4
w-questions 8.2

yes/no questions 8.2
yet 3.4; 24.14
you 20.1,4
your, yours 20.5
yourself, yourselves 20.7,8; 28.5

Glossary

This *Glossary* gives the meaning of words which may be hard to understand. If the word is not in the Glossary, look in the *Index* on pages 154–158.

active ▷ **passive**
adjective In the sentence *It's a big car,* the word *big* is an adjective. An adjective describes a noun. ▷ 23.1
adverb In the sentence *They're playing happily,* the word *happily* is an adverb. ▷ 24
apostrophe This is an apostrophe: ' ▷ 37.4
article The articles are *a/an* and *the.* ▷ 19
auxiliary verb helping verb: *be, have* and *do* ▷ 5.1
basic form The basic form of the verb has no ending, e. g. *go, play.*
clause *We can go in the car if it rains* is a sentence. *We can go in the car* is the **main clause** and *if it rains* is a **sub clause.** Sometimes a sentence is a main clause only, e.g. *We can go in the car.*
complement In the sentence *She's a doctor,* the phrase *a doctor* is the complement. The complement describes the subject.
compound a word which we form from two or more other words, e.g. *milkman* (milk + man), *somewhere* (some + where)
conjunction E.g. (in sub clauses) *when, if, because;* (in main clauses) *and, but, or* ▷ 27.1
consonant The letters *b,c,d,f,g,h,j,k,l,m,n,p,q,r,s,t,v,w,x,y* [j] and *z* and the sounds of these letters ▷ **vowel**
defining relative clause ▷ 22.12
definite *Ten minutes* is a **definite** time; we know how many minutes. *A few minutes* is an **indefinite** time; we do not know exactly how many minutes.
direct object In the sentence *The boy gave his father a book,* the noun phrase *a book* is the **direct object,** and the noun phrase *his father* is the **indirect object.** ▷ 1.1,4
direct speech ▷ **reported speech**
double do something twice (= x 2)
-ed form ▷ **past participle**
emphasis (Adjective: **emphatic)** making a word or words more important ▷ 28
ending In the noun *books, -s* is the plural ending.
end position In the sentence *We go out sometimes,* the word *sometimes* is in end position. ▷ 24.9
exclamation a sentence that is spoken suddenly and with feeling, e.g. *Stop! That's great!*
express put an idea into words, find the words for what you want to say
falling intonation the voice going down ▷ 39
female Girls and women are **female;** boys and men are **male.**
formal Friendly, everyday conversations are **informal;** business letters are more **formal.**
front position In the sentence *Sometimes we go out,* the word *sometimes* is in front position. ▷ 24.9
full verb a normal verb, e.g. *look, come;* not an auxiliary or modal verb
future the time that has not yet come, the time after now
imperative a form of the verb that we use to give orders, e.g. *Wait a minute. Come here.* ▷ 6.1
indefinite ▷ **definite**
indirect object ▷ **direct object**
infinitive the basic form of the verb, e.g. *wait, come.* The infinitive is often with *to,* e.g. *to wait, to come.* ▷ 14
informal ▷ **formal**
-ing form form of a verb with *-ing,* e.g *opening, walking* ▷ 15
intonation the speaker's voice (the sounds which the speaker makes) going up and down
irregular ▷ **regular**
limited meaning a narrow meaning, not a wide or a general meaning
limited number not a very large number
linking word a conjunction (e.g. *if, and*) or a word or phrase which makes a link or a bridge between two sentences (e.g. *therefore, on the other hand*) ▷ 27
main clause ▷ **clause**
male ▷ **female**
mid position In the sentence *We sometimes go out,* the word *sometimes* is in mid position. ▷ 24.9
modal verb E.g. *can, must* ▷ 7.1
negative A statement with *not* or *n't* is **negative,** e.g. *I haven't got a watch.* ▷ 8.1 Other statements are **positive,** e.g. *There's a clock on the wall.*

non-defining relative clause ▷ 22.12
noun In the sentence *The boys are in the garden,* the words *boys* and *garden* are nouns.
object ▷ **direct object**
order E.g. *Come here.* ▷ 34.1
passive *The police arrested the man* is an **active** sentence. *The man was arrested* is a **passive** sentence. ▷ 10.1
past the time that is already over, the time before now
past participle the -ed form of a verb, e.g. *opened, walked;* some forms are irregular, e.g. *seen, come.*
perception ▷ **verb of perception**
person 1st person = *I, we;* 2nd person = *you,* 3rd person = *he, she, it, they.*
phrase a group of words but not a full clause or sentence, e.g. *the red car* (a noun phrase), *is walking* (a verb phrase), *before dinner* (a prepositional phrase)
plural more than one thing ▷ **singular**
polite It is polite to say *please* and *thank you.*
positive ▷ **negative**
possess (Noun: **possession**) have, own; *We possess a car.* = We have a car. (It's our car; it belongs to us.)
preposition E.g. *in, on, under, at, to* ▷ 25
present the time now, at this moment
present participle the -ing form of a verb, e.g. *opening, walking* ▷ 17
pronoun E.g. *you, it* ▷ 20
pronounce (Noun: **pronunciation**) say words correctly
punctuation E.g. a comma (,) or full stop (.) ▷ 37
quantifier a word that tells us about quantity, e.g. *some, every, much* ▷ 20
quantity an amount or number (how much, how many)
question tag In the sentence *It's Monday today, isn't it?* the phrase *isn't it?* is a question tag. ▷ 8.5
question word *what, who, whose, which, where, when, why* and *how* ▷ 21
regular the same as others; The words *boys* and *girls* are nouns with **regular** plural endings in *-s.* The word *children* is an **irregular** plural form.
relative clause In the sentence *That's the girl who came first,* the clause *who came first* is a relative clause. ▷ 22
repeat say again
reported speech The sentence *"I can come"* is **direct speech**. In the sentence *He says he can come,* the clause *he can come* is a reported clause (**reported speech**). ▷ 12.1
rising intonation the voice going up ▷ 39
singular one thing ▷ **plural**
sound (noun) something that we can hear
speech speaking, talking
spelling writing words correctly
statement a sentence which gives information (e.g. *The game is on Saturday. I don't like football.*); not a question or an order
stress speaking a word (or part of a word) more loudly than other words
sub clause E.g. *when I see you, if she comes;* A **sub clause** (= subordinate clause) begins with a conjunction, e.g. *when, if, because,* but not with *and, or* or *but.* **Relative clauses** and **reported clauses** are special kinds of sub clauses. ▷ **clause**
subject In the sentence *The man opened the door,* the noun phrase *the man* is the subject.
tag ▷ **question tag**
tense a form of the verb which tells us when something happens, e.g. in the present, the past or the future
verb In the sentence *I read the newspaper every day,* the word *read* is a verb.
verb-noun a verb form which we use as a noun, e.g. *I like* reading.
verb of perception E.g. *see, hear, notice, smell*
voiced/voiceless **Voiced** sounds are all the vowel sounds (e.g. [iː], [e], [aʊ]) and the consonant sounds [b], [d], [g], [z], [ʒ], [dʒ], [v], [ð], [l], [r], [m], [n], and [ŋ]. **Voiceless** sounds are the consonant sounds [p], [t], [k], [s], [ʃ], [tʃ], [f] and [θ].
vowel the letters *a,e,i,o* and *u* and the sounds of these letters ▷ **consonant**
w-question a question that begins *What/Who/Whose/Which/Where/When/Why/How* ...?
yes/no question a question that we can answer with *yes* or *no*